The La Iun

J N Harris

Enjoy!

(signature)

notreallybooks

Copyright J N Harris 2018

First published in Great Britain in 2018 by
notreallybooks
Suite 111 Dorset House
Duke Street
Chelmsford CM1 1TB

Cover design by Jem Butcher

Printed and bound in Great Britain by Clays Ltd. Bungay, Suffolk

The right of J N Harris to be identified as author of this work has
been asserted by him in accordance with the Copyright, Designs
and Patents Act 1988

A CIP catalogue record for this book is available from the British
Library

ISBN 978 – 0 – 9552129 – 4 – 9

For
Fran and Nic

As the first light of dawn crept through the trees a young girl watched a group of soldiers carrying their captives onto the open back of a lorry. When the captives were covered by a tarpaulin and the sides of the lorry were lifted and locked into place she asked one of them, "Have you got permission to do this?" He shook his head and, with a wink, said, "We do everything our masters tell us, but we don't tell our masters everything we do."

1

It was the worst day of my life. (At least up to then. I might have had worse since but we'll come to that later.)

It started with one of the girls from Year 11 coming in while we were making the beds and accusing me of stealing something – I can't even remember what now – and after a couple of minutes of her accusing me and me denying it and everyone gathering round and gawping she leaned her head back so she was looking down her nose at me and in a loud and snotty voice said 'A liar and a crook, just like her father'. With that she spun round on her heels and started to walk out.

I'm afraid I lost it.

I did a flying drop kick from behind and flattened her to the ground. There was a bit of blood and a lot of screaming and her friends took her off to the medical wing while my lot just stood and watched and didn't do a thing, which was typical.

So I wasn't surprised when I got dragged out of assembly and told to wait outside The Beak's office, and didn't suspect anything as I walked along the corridor getting funny looks from some of the admin staff and some of the nuns as I walked past them.

The corridor outside The Beak's office is long and draughty. The main entrance to the school is at the other end and every time anyone goes in or out through the front door this huge gust of wind appears from nowhere and rushes down the corridor like a freight train. She leaves you sitting on the hard bench outside her office for ages deliberately to make you feel cold, abandoned and very alone.

And it works.

Even if you're sitting there with friends you never feel like talking 'cos you know you're in trouble and you suspect she'll hear anything you say, and you never feel more like wanting to phone home, or better still actually be home. It's the one place in the school that's guaranteed to make you feel homesick even if you never feel homesick normally. It's where you remember her saying in your first assembly that however we might feel about being there we have NOT been abandoned by our parents, we've just been left in her care.

It's the one place in the whole school where you can't help but feel that actually, yes, you have been abandoned by your parents.

Finally the door opened and her blonde and skinny PA (who obviously thinks she's glamorous but who's really just a very blonde and far too skinny wannabe model who never made it) appeared with her slick smile and said "You may see The Head now." She always says that and I always think What? Just the head? Where's the rest of her? But I never actually said it out loud and now I really, really, wish I did when I had the chance.

She walked out and I walked in and the big heavy door clunked behind me. The Beak was signing some papers and ignored me for a few seconds which seemed like minutes and then without looking up at me pointed to the chair facing her desk and said "Sit down, please, Camille." There was something about her tone of voice that told me this wasn't about the fight that morning. This was something else. Something worse.

She put the cap on her pen and put it down, put her hands together as if she was about to pray and then looked at me.

She looked at me for what seemed like a whole minute (try it – it's a long time) before saying, "I'm afraid I've some rather bad news." My heart leaped. What? Who? Had someone died? Phones had been banned after the incident with the Viola teacher and the yoghurt (which was honestly nothing to do with me, although I admit I knew who was responsible and I did find it funny, so that was enough to get me in trouble as well) so I hadn't spoken to either of my parents for over a week and it could have been anything or anyone.

She took a deep breath and said, "I'm afraid that, despite continued efforts on our part to be both reasonable and accommodating, your parents have still not been able or willing to settle the increasingly large account they have with this school."

"Sorry?" I said.

"Your father has not paid a penny of your fees for eighteen months," she explained. "Did you not know?" I shook my head. I had no idea.

"So who's been paying them?" I asked, rather stupidly.

"No one," she replied. "And I'm afraid we've reached the point where we have to draw a line. 'Thus far, and no further', as they say."

I'm ashamed to admit that I still didn't twig what was going on, but then she spelt it out.

"Yesterday afternoon I had a phone call from the police asking if I had any idea as to your father's whereabouts. When I told them I had no idea but that the bursar had been trying to contact him about the money he owed the school the officer laughed and said something about having to join the back of a very long queue. Apparently your father owes a lot of money to a lot of people and now he seems to have completely disappeared."

Don't be silly, I thought, no one completely disappears, you just don't know where he is and you're not clever enough to find him. But what I said, rather pathetically, was, "What about my mum?"

"We don't seem to be able to contact her either," she said. Something in her tone made me realise she really was enjoying this. She smiled her horrible fake smile, the one she uses when she's pretending to be kind and sweet in front of parents. It got my hackles up and I started to get defensive.

"So what can I do about it?" I tried to sound tough, as if I didn't care, but my voice cracked slightly as I spoke and I knew I'd blown it.

"When we've finished this conversation you can go and pack your bags."

"What?"

"I'm afraid this is the point at which we must go our separate ways. When you're ready someone will take you to the station."

"You can't just chuck me out!" my voice was louder than I'd meant it to be. She raised her eyebrows slightly as if to say 'try me'. "Don't you have a – what's it called – a duty of care?" I asked. "You can't just chuck me out on the streets!"

"Someone will take you to the station and your grandmother will meet you at Oxenholme. We spoke last night and again this morning. A charming and delightful woman."

That was when I knew things really were starting to fall apart. Charming and delightful? My grandmother? A lot of people have said a lot of things about my grandmother over the years but no one in living memory has ever called her 'charming and delightful'. She's a dangerous psychopath with slightly batty tendencies which some people, I admit, sometimes find endearing but CHARMING AND DELIGHTFUL? She's fierce! She's savage! She can make grown men stop in their tracks just by looking at them and grown women start snivelling when she aims her cutting comments and ironic praise at them. She's quite possibly the only person in the world my dad is genuinely scared of and she's so ungrandmotherlike that she refuses even to be called by that word and insists I call her by her proper name. Then again, I suppose someone like The Beak would find her charming and delightful because they have so much in common.

I can't even remember the rest of the conversation or the walk back up to the dorm. I didn't see anyone all the way up there but there was a card on my bed from Miss Kimble wishing me luck so the news had obviously spread. I think it was the first time in my life I was really in shock. I felt kind of numb but at the same time a sense of shame I'd never felt before. It suddenly felt as if the whole world knew that my dad wasn't always what he seemed. Unlike my grandmother he really was charming and delightful but somehow I always knew there was another side to him, even though I'd never actually seen it myself. Even with someone you love as much as I loved my dad you know when there's something else, even if you don't see it yourself. It was as if the rest of the world had suddenly seen through the charm and saw him for what he really was – or what they thought he really was. I knew they were wrong, but I knew I couldn't argue or do anything to change their opinion and that made me feel bad.

I remembered what that silly cow in Year 11 had said about him earlier that morning and I wanted to go back and kick her even harder.

When I got to the main entrance, Harry, one of the groundsmen, was waiting for me. Through the windows by the main door I could see the mini bus he drove parked outside. "All ready?" he asked, so he knew as well. I nodded. "We're just waiting for Miss Kimble."

"She's got a lesson," I said.

"Someone must be covering for her 'cos she's coming as well," he shrugged. He took my bags and put them in the back and then we stood in an uncomfortable silence waiting for Miss K.

Finally he asked, "So what did you do?"

"What makes you think I've done anything?" I said, rather too defensively.

"Because if you're being packed off to the station at this time in the morning it isn't to go and collect a medal, is it?"

2

Not much was said in the mini bus. I was still in shock and subdued and I think the other two knew that and were trying to be helpful.

We pulled up in the station car park and as Harry got out to get my bags Miss Kimble got out as well. "See you later," Harry nodded to her as he got back in. "Take care," he called out to me and then drove off.

"Are you going shopping?" I asked.

"Don't be silly, I'm coming with you."

"What? All the way to Euston?" She nodded. "You don't need to," I said.

"Duty of care," she smiled and I knew The Beak had told her about our conversation. "I have to see you on to the platform at Euston."

"Yeah, but you'd rather go shopping, wouldn't you?" I gave her my best We-Girls-Know-Really smile.

"Of course I'd rather go shopping but can you imagine what would happen if I got back to school with a bundle of carrier bags only to be told that your Grandmother had phoned to say you hadn't arrived?"

"Oh, come on," I said "I bet even The Beak bunked off now and then when she was younger…"

A smile crept across her face and she said softly, "I somehow doubt Sister Moira was ever young and I'm certain she's never bunked off anywhere in her entire life. I've been given strict instructions, and I have no choice but to follow them."

"Isn't that what the guards at the concentration camps said?"

"Let us continue the analogy," she smiled again. "Be glad you've escaped. Don't mess it up!"

"Okay, what about lunch first?" I asked. "I know a couple of really good places we could go to." This was true, but it was also true that I didn't have any money so it was a bluff and the look on her face told me she knew it was. She handed me a ticket and pointed to the barriers. "Walk!" she said, admittedly with a twinkle in her eye.

So I walked.

St. Dunstan's is in London's commuter belt but the commuters had all gone off to work by then so the train was fairly empty and Liverpool Street station was quite calm compared to what it can be like. By the time we got on the tube the workers had all been decanted and replaced by middle aged American tourists (you can always spot them even before you hear their accents 'cos they always wear trainers and bum bags) so at least that meant we could get a seat.

We didn't say much. I was watching the tourists and I think she was watching me. That was one of the things I liked about her. Any other member of staff would have felt the need to 'engage in conversation' all the way between school and Euston, which would have been tiresome for both of us and potentially embarrassing for me, but Miss K wasn't like that. If I was working on something in the art room she'd just leave me to it and if I wanted to carry on working over lunch time or after school she was probably the only member of staff who'd trust me to be left alone. The science department certainly wouldn't do that. To be fair, if I'd been a science teacher I wouldn't have trusted me alone in a lab with stuff that could be poisonous or explosive, but the art rooms were different. They were the only rooms where I was never tempted to muck about. It's not that I'm brilliant at art – quite the opposite, probably – but I did try hard and I loved the calm of the art rooms. The trouble was, however hard I tried I just couldn't get what I saw in my head down on paper. I can sketch and draw something in front of me perfectly well, but whenever I try to do something out of my own imagination it just doesn't come out anything like what I had in mind. Everyone else looks at it and says "Oh, that's really good," but I know it isn't 'cos it isn't what I was trying to get. Miss Kimble always said relax and it'll sort itself out but I never could so it never did, at least not how I wanted it to. I suppose it's like when you really love a sport but you're just not good enough to make it into the team: it doesn't stop you loving the sport and it doesn't stop you trying. That's how I am with painting.

We got to Euston with about twenty minutes left before my train was due to leave. I tried once more, just for the hell of it. "If you've changed your mind about lunch I could get the next one."

"I have a surprise for you," she said as she opened her big tote bag with a bit of a flourish and produced a St. Dunstan's packed lunch. "Oh, you're joking!" I moaned as I looked inside the brown paper bag and saw the inevitable clingfilmed cheese roll made with leather cheese and three day old bread, the mini packet of digestives that were already broken and past their best before date, the room temperature yoghurt and the carton of warm, crappy sharp orange juice. I held the juice out towards her. "You should keep this stuff in the art room. It can strip paint, so God knows what it does to your teeth!"

She opened her purse, held out a fiver and nodded towards the food hall as she took the packed lunch from me. "Go and get what you want. No alcohol. Be quick!"

"Thanks, Ma'm!" I almost ran with relief and got something half way decent. When I got back she waved away the change and handed me another fiver for the journey and a small carrier bag. "What's this?" I asked.

"Something for you to read on the train."

"I've got my phone."

"Don't be such a philistine," she smiled. I took the book out of the bag. 'The Catcher in the Rye' by J D Salinger.

"Never heard of it," I said.

"Nevertheless you'll love it." She took a step forward and gave me a hug, which took me by surprise and actually brought a lump to my throat. "Be careful," she said. "Look after yourself, try not to get into trouble, let me know how you're getting on and above all do not stop drawing and painting – you're better than you think you are. Now off you go." She let go of me and half patted and half pushed me on my way. I looked over my shoulder as I got to the entrance to the platform and she was still there watching me.

"I'm not moving from here until that train has gone!" she called, as if I was thinking of making a run for it.

Honestly, as if!

There was no escape.

3

I was glad of the book. I realised listening to music all the way to Oxenholme would run down my battery and if I was going to use my newly returned phone it ought to be to talk to people. I tried my mum but all I got was voicemail. Several times. I tried my dad but it made that noise you get when a number no longer exists, which was worrying. I tried phoning friends but of course they were all in school so I left some messages and then, out of a combination of boredom and courtesy, I phoned my Grandmother.

"Hello, Joan," I said, "it's Camille. I'm on the train."

"How terribly original," she said.

"Sorry?"

"Everybody who ever makes a call from a train begins by telling whoever they're calling that they're on the train. That much should be obvious because of the background noise and the quality of the signal, and yet people persist in stating the unbelievably obvious in a way that forces everyone else on the train to overhear their mundane conversation. I'd expect something a little more original from my own granddaughter."

"Well, yes, but what I meant was -"

"I'm very busy just now, Camille. We'll have plenty of time to talk once you get here," she said. "See you at the station" and the line went dead. Oh, great, I thought. This is going to be so much fun.

So I spent the rest of the journey reading. Well that's not strictly true: I spent a large part of the journey watching my fellow passengers chugging up and down the aisle to the buffet car or the toilets, and I spent a fair amount of time looking at the scenery whizzing past and noticing how it changed as we got further north. I thought about sketching some of the impressions I got as the train whizzed past things, but all the stuff I'd need was at the bottom of my case and I didn't want the hassle of unpacking it all just to end up looking pretentious.

And I spent some of the time just day dreaming and nearly nodding off. But I did spend the rest of the time reading, and it didn't take me long to work out why Miss Kimble had bought me that particular book. It's great. So great that I suggest when you've finished reading this you read that, if you haven't already.

Since the train wasn't exactly heaving I was surprised by how many people got off at Oxenholme. I suppose I shouldn't have been: It was April, Oxenholme is one of the main stations for the Lake District and the Lake District is one of the most beautiful parts of the country and lots of people want to go there.

Just not me.

I let everyone else get off first – they were looking forward to it, I wasn't – and after a minute or two the station cleared itself of tourists and I could see my Grandmother by the entrance. I hadn't seen her for years but she didn't look a day older. She was tall and had a straight back and had a way of standing that always made her look as if she owned wherever she was – even a railway station. I remembered how, if I'd been naughty when I was little, she could scare the life out of me just by looking at me and not even saying anything.

She smiled when she saw me but didn't move from the spot. I lugged my bags over to where she was standing and she presented her cheeks for me to kiss. I wondered if a firm hand shake might have been more appropriate.

Or a Nazi salute.

"How are you?" I asked

"I'm fine, but I can do without this kind of stress

at my age," she said in a way that made me feel as if it was all my fault and I'd be the death of her before I finished. I tried to lighten the situation by making a joke. "Don't blame me, blame my Ma for marrying my Pa!"

"Don't think I haven't done that many times over the years," she said as she walked out of the station and down the road with me struggling to keep up.

I noticed a sign pointing to the car park but she kept walking down the road.

"Isn't that the way?" I asked.

"I don't park there, it's daylight robbery," she said. "We're just down here." So I followed as fast as I could. Would it have killed her to at least carry the lighter bag?

Her car was a nice, new, shiny blue Land Rover. Business must be good, I thought. It occurred to me that she could probably have paid my school fees and stopped me getting thrown out, but she wouldn't because sending me to boarding school had been my dad's idea and she hadn't agreed with it so she'd have said it was nothing to do with her. She flicked a switch on her keyring and the boot opened automatically. She nodded towards the boot and by the time I'd thrown my stuff in she was sitting in the car. As I reached for the handle to the boot it quietly closed itself. Business must be really good, I thought.

"It's good to see you, Camille," she said as I climbed in and closed the door, "but I do wish it was under different circumstances. I'm really quite cross with your parents."

"Have you heard from them?" I asked as I fastened my seat belt. She started the engine and put it into gear.

"Strangely enough I haven't. And I say strangely enough because I usually hear quite a lot from your mother when your father is in a spot of bother of some kind. It usually means he needs to 'borrow' money from me which I know I'll never see again. The fact that I haven't heard from her and they both seem to have disappeared suggests this time it's serious." She waited for another car to go past and then put her foot down and hared off down the road.

"Woa!" I said as I felt myself pushed back into the seat, "D'ya rob a bank?" and as soon as I said it I knew how she'd respond and could have kicked myself when she said, "I leave that sort of thing to your father." I realised I was going to have to work hard to make this tolerable for me at least, if not for both of us.

There is a main road you can take for most of the way from the station to my Grandmother's house but within minutes she'd turned off that and onto what was little more than a dirt track. "Why've we come off the main road?" I asked.

"That's for the tourists," she replied. "This way's quicker – and much more fun!" She put her foot down hard on the accelerator and I remembered that her dad – my great grandfather – had been a rally driver and I guessed he'd taught her a thing or two. We bounced up and down over hills and potholes and went down some parts of the road that were so narrow I found myself breathing in as if it would help us squeeze through, and couldn't understand how she didn't scrape the sides of the car.

She swung around sharp bends and over cattle grids like a kid on a Go Kart. I was so taken up with the way she was driving I didn't really notice the scenery until she started pointing things out to me, but then I began to see why why mum always said it was the most beautiful part of the country. The sky was a deep blue, the afternoon sun was shining down on impossibly green fields and there seemed to be sheep and lambs everywhere.

Suddenly we were back on a main road with lots of other cars, some towing caravans, some towing boats, some with bikes strapped to the roof or the back and in some cases both. It looked as if the whole world had arrived for an early Easter holiday. There were thousands of wild daffodils at the sides of the road and cafes with cars and motorbikes parked outside. I saw a flash of blue through the trees as we drove past the edge of a lake and asked, "Is that Coniston?"

"Windermere," she shook her head. "Where the noisy people go."

"How do you mean?"

"There used to be lots of speedboats and noisy parties on big boats," she explained. "They put a stop to all that a few years ago with a ten miles per hour speed limit, but it still manages to be noisy and there always seems to be a party of some kind going on."

"Sounds good to me," I said.

"Where we are is much nicer," she said. "Much quieter."

Oh dear, I thought. That's a shame.

She turned onto another dirt track through a gap I didn't even see coming and within seconds it was as if we'd just had a glimpse into another universe and then been slammed back into one where we were alone. There were no other people. No cars, bikes, boats or caravans. Just green hills, sunshine, and an awful lot of sheep.

"It does all look lovely," I said, trying to sound enthusiastic but already missing the noise and bustle.

"It's not always like this," she warned. "When it rains – and you may remember from when you were little it rains a lot – it can be a bit grim. But it has to rain: we have to keep the lakes topped up."

It was so peaceful, quiet and sunny it didn't look as if it could ever be grim.

We drove past groups of houses, not even enough to call a village, most of which seemed to be made of the same grey stone and slate. There were tractors and Land Rovers coming in and out of farms and one farm at the bottom of a hill had a big hand painted sign which said:

Your satnav is wrong.
Turn round and go back now!

"That's Arnold," she explained. "He got fed up with people driving up to the top of the hill only to find his farm and no road down the other way. They had to turn round in the farmyard and go all the way back down again, but of course some people complained because they thought he was being miserable."

"When he was really trying to help them?"

"No," she laughed, "he was being miserable. There is a road down the other side but he'd blocked it off years ago and everyone had forgotten about it until the satnavs told them it was there. For the next couple of weeks everyone sang 'The Grand Old Duke of York' whenever he walked into the pub."

"Huh?"

"He marched them up to the top of the hill and he marched them down again."

"Oh, right!" I realised I'd been a bit slow on the uptake. "So do they still do that when he walks into the pub?"

"No," she smiled at the memory. "He got so fed up of it he offered to buy everyone in the pub a drink if they promised to stop. So while half the people in the pub were standing around thanking him the other half were running up and down the road knocking on people's doors telling them the drinks were on Arnold. It had never happened before and will never happen again so they wanted to make the most of it. He's a mean old so – and – so, so the pub was heaving that night."

"Why were they running up and down the road telling people?" I asked. "They could just have phoned everyone."

She laughed again. "You can't get a signal for your phone around here, silly girl!" She obviously thought this was really funny but it hadn't occurred to me. No signal? What the hell was I going to do without a phone?

"Here we are!" she announced as we turned a corner and started to go down a hill I hadn't noticed we'd gone up. I could suddenly see almost the whole of the lake. It was long and thin with an island in the middle and there didn't seem to be anyone or anything anywhere near the lake. The water was so smooth and calm that it reflected the blue of the sky above like a mirror. She turned sharply through a set of gates I hadn't even noticed and there in front of us was her house.

Cottage.

Big cottage.

Mansion.

I don't know, whatever you want to call it, really.

Home.

Built out of Lakeland slate with matt green paintwork on the doors and windows, flowers along the path that led to the front door and a neat little garden all around it and down to the lake. Perhaps it was the light and warmth of the afternoon sun but it didn't seem as gothic and rambling as I remembered. In fact it looked quite welcoming, and made me feel a little better.

"Beautiful, isn't she?" My Grandmother asked.

"What, the house?"

"No, the lake, silly!"

I realised I'd reached the end of a journey in more ways than one. I was hundreds of miles away from a school I'd probably never go back to and hundreds of miles away from all my friends. In front of me was a big old house I barely remembered from childhood and a big, and older, lake beyond that.

"They're both lovely," I said quietly, feeling another lump forming in my throat.

"I'm glad you like it," she said. "For a while, at least, this is your home."

The lake was beautiful, the house was nothing like as bad as I imagined, and my Grandmother didn't seem to be quite as awful as I remembered (or my dad had told me).

But home? With no signal?

4

As we got out of the car the front door opened and Uncle Frank came to help with our bags. I say 'Uncle Frank' because that's what everyone calls him but he wasn't really my uncle and at that point I had no idea whose uncle, if anybody's, he actually was, or what relation he was to anyone else. He was always just Uncle Frank. He was about six feet tall and as bald as a coot. (What is a coot anyway? And where did that expression come from? Ahhhh… just think – I could've looked it up if there'd been a signal.) He also had the biggest grin I've ever seen on a grown up, and it was there most of the time. Even when he wasn't actually grinning he looked happy. He always looked as if he'd just pulled the world's most amazing practical joke and completely got away with it.

Which, although I didn't know it at the time, I suppose he had in a way.

"Now then, lass, where've you been? We've missed you!" he said as he lifted one of my bags out of the car and I realised it must have been at least six or seven years since I'd been to the house. I thought of all the times he'd made me laugh when

I was little or made me something to eat when I got back from playing outside, and as I followed him into the house, what with one thing and another, I began to think this might not turn out so bad after all. Even though he hadn't seen me for years at least he hadn't said anything as crass as 'Oooh, haven't you grown?' which most people who think they're grown up tell me and I absolutely hate.

"You know which room she's in, I take it?" my Grandmother called after him.

"The same one you used to stay in when you were a la'lun," he told me over his shoulder.

"What's a la'lun?" I asked. My Grandmother snorted at my ignorance of the local dialect while Frank replied, "La'l is small. You're the small one. The la'lun. Well, the youngest anyway. Maybe not so small now."

Agh! He blew it!

We turned a corner and he opened the door to the room with his elbow. "Here you are lass, room sweet room. You might notice we've made a few changes since you were last here." He dropped the bag onto the bed, winked at me and said, "It's lovely to have you back. I'll see you at supper," and left us to it, closing the door behind him.

I looked around, trying to remember the room as it was when I was little. It was big, and a bit ramshackle in those days. So ramshackle, in fact, that Joan used drawing pins and a ball of wool to draw a line right down one wall, across the middle of the room and up the opposite wall. One side I was to keep clean and tidy, the other I could do whatever I liked with. So I did. There was paint and toys all over it and there was paint all over the toys. But not the books. I had to keep the books in what she called the 'civilized' side. But you wouldn't know any of that to look at it now. It was a comfortable room in mostly shades of blue and grey with a big bed on one side, a sofa on the other and a huge walk in shower room with slate floors and walls and a power shower. "Wow! This is amazing!" I said. And it was. After the cramped cubicles at school this was five star luxury. And then I noticed a pile of sketch books and different sets of pencils on a table. "Are these for me?" I asked.

"Of course. I thought you might find them useful."

"Oh, thanks, that's really kind," I said as I looked at them. "And they're really good quality."

"Buying cheap always turns out to be a waste of money," she said.

"And the room is just amazing!" I repeated. I think I was what they call overcompensating, or something. I was trying to ingratiate myself, and trying too hard.

"I'm glad you like it," she said as she sat on the sofa. "We want you to be comfortable and, whatever I think of your parents at the moment, I'm glad you're here. I've hardly seen you in the last few years and it's going to be good to get to know the new you."

"New me?" I asked.

"You're hardly the child who stayed here all those years ago," she said. "You're a young woman now and I want to get to know that young woman." I felt flattered. I know that sounds silly but I did. I don't know about you, but I reckon most adults who knew you as a little kid always see you at least in part as that little kid. Don't get me wrong, that can be useful if you know how to play it, but it can also be a bit limiting. But then she spoiled things by saying, "You are, however, going to have to earn your keep. I've spoken to a friend in the County Council who says all the local schools are pretty much full and it would be a bit of a nuisance all round if you were to join one of them at this stage in the year. The nearest one's six miles away so we'd have to arrange transport and we don't know how long you're going to be here yet so she said they could regard you as being home schooled for the rest of the academic year. But you will have to be at school somewhere in September."

"I don't have to go to school until September? But it's the beginning of April – that means a whole four months off school!"

"Five," she corrected me. "Maths was never your strong point. But this is not going to be an extended holiday. I'll be setting you things to do and you might have to help out at the hotel if we get particularly busy."

Oh, did I mention she owns a hotel? Well, she and Frank between them. It's a few miles away, and they don't like to live 'over the shop' as she puts it, but they own what's called a 'boutique' hotel. Which means it's small, exclusive and quite expensive. It's the kind of hotel where the rooms don't just have 'tea and coffee making facilities', they have those posh coffee pod machines and packets of organic cookies. And they actively discourage riff-raff from staying there. Which, I suppose, is why I didn't get a room there.

"What would I be doing at the hotel?" I asked.

"Whatever you turn out to be good at," she shrugged. "Cleaning rooms, preparing vegetables or washing up in the kitchen. If you can manage to carry things without dropping them and smile at the guests I might even let you to loose in the restaurant, we'll just have to see." She paused and then said, "Now, there are one or two other things we need to get sorted out." By which she meant 'lay down the law', which she proceeded to do.

"Frank and I get up early in the mornings. One or other of us usually goes for a walk around the lake before making breakfast. So I need you to be up, showered, dressed and down for breakfast by seven o'clock every morning because we've usually left for the hotel by seven thirty."

"At school we get up at seven and then shower and stuff…" my half hearted attempt at protest fizzled out to nothing when I saw the look on her face. This would mean getting up at half past six every morning. She was right about this not being a holiday.

"What about the weekends?" I asked.

"The same."

"But we get a half hour lie in at the weekends," I pointed out.

"At school you did, but you're not at school now." That much was becoming quite clear. And I thought the nuns were hard on us! By now she was getting into her stride. "You'll be responsible for keeping your room and shower room spotless. Geraldine comes over here after she's finished at the hotel but I can't afford to have staff wasting their time cleaning up after you, so I mean spotless and I will check," she emphasised as I quietly nodded agreement.

Agreement or submission, I'm not sure which.

"When you're at the hotel, whether it be working or just visiting, I need you to be polite and courteous at all times to guests and staff. I can't afford to lose either because of the antics of an adolescent brat."

"I am not an adolescent brat!" I really did object to that.

"I should hope not, but I need to make it clear from the outset that you will not be one while you are under this roof. Is that understood?" I nodded. "Now, while you're here you have a degree of freedom," (Really? I wondered) "but all freedoms have to be restricted."

"Isn't that an oxymoron?" I asked.

"Only if you're a moron," she said flatly.

"But you can't have restricted freedom, it's not freedom if it's restricted."

She sighed and said, "We don't have time for a philosophical discussion. You'll just have to take my word for it: there is no such thing as absolute freedom, it simply wouldn't work." I opened my mouth to speak but she didn't give me the chance.

"You can go anywhere you want within the house, the garden, around the lake, the village and the surrounding area." Then she paused and said, "But you must not go into the boat house, and you mustn't use the boat even when it's just moored at the edge of the lake. Boats are dangerous, and water is dangerous. And you absolutely must not, under any circumstances – and I cannot emphasise this enough – go on to the island in the middle of the lake."

I hadn't even thought of doing so until she mentioned it.

"Why not?" I asked.

"It's privately owned and dangerous."

"I thought you owned it."

"I do, and that's how I know it's dangerous."

"Wow!" I said. "In what way is it dangerous? Is it like Area 51 with crashed UFOs and stuff?" I was hoping she might find that slightly amusing, an attempt to lighten the mood, but she saw it for the sarcasm it really was.

"Don't be facetious," she said. "I am serious. You must NOT go onto the island. It's unbelievably overgrown, uneven and swampy. If you're not torn to shreds you'll trip up and break a leg or get stuck in one of the boggier parts. Either way you'll be unable to attract attention or do anything to save yourself. You'll be stranded there until you rot."

"You could come looking for me," I suggested.

"What would be the point? That would simply be throwing one life away after another."

Gosh! I thought. My Grandmother cares about me such a lot!

"Now I've got a very busy day tomorrow but Frank has offered to take you into town and get you kitted out with decent walking gear. I want you to take a walk every day, unless the weather is atrocious. Whilst you're here you might as well come to appreciate your surroundings, and it'll help get you fit."

"I am fit!"

"I doubt you're as fit as I am and I'm at least twice your age." She raised an eyebrow to tell me not to argue and I was beginning to suspect that she might have a sense of humour after all. She was more like five times my age. "Walking properly around here requires energy, strength and stamina – far more than you get from a game of netball a couple of times a week."

I wasn't going to argue with that. I hated PE lessons and netball always struck me as just a wimp version of basketball. The only game I liked was Lacrosse but they banned that when I was in Year 7 for the very reason I liked it: it was dangerous.

"Once you get the hang of walking – "

I sniggered. I know. Pathetic. Couldn't help myself.

"I've been doing it for a while now, Gran," I told her.

"Don't call me 'Gran'," she almost snapped. "Once you get the hang of it you'll want to go further afield, which is all well and good, but you must make sure you let either me or Frank know where you'll be going and what time you're likely to be back."

"I thought the point of walking was for the freedom. Wandering lonely as a cloud and all that."

"We've discussed this already. There is no such thing as freedom. Least of all in this house."

"We didn't actually discuss it – you just laid down the law."

"And that's the way it's gonna be, partner," she said in a phoney American accent which was mildly amusing. "I'm the Sheriff round these parts."

"So I have to tell you if I'm going for a walk?"

"Up on the fells the weather can change dramatically within minutes," she said, "even at this time of year. It can sometimes become really dangerous."

"Isn't there a mountain rescue team?" I asked.

"Some of that team are good friends of mine and I'd never live it down if I had to call on them to rescue my own granddaughter."

"Carry on like this and I'm not going to leave the house," I said. "Boats are dangerous, water's dangerous. I can't go onto the island in case I get stuck there and die a slow and wretched death in the mud, and I can't go for a walk for fear of hypothermia – you're starting to scare me!" She wasn't really but I wanted to appeal to her maternal and protective side.

Or at least to see if she had one.

"There's nothing to be scared of, as long as you're sensible," she said. "Most people who come here just want to drive around a bit, look at the scenery, go for a walk and then eat and drink, which is fine. They're enjoying themselves, the locals are making money, everyone's happy. But there's always some idiot who decides to go for a walk without the right clothing, food and water, or even a compass, and when they're half way up one of the fells the light goes or the weather turns and they're stuffed. I don't believe you're one of those idiots and I don't want to be proved wrong."

Ah… so she did have a maternal side after all! Sort of. But then it disappeared just as quickly.

"There's plenty for you to do around here, and plenty for you to read. I want you to make sure you do not use the internet for more than half an hour a day."

"Half an hour?" This place was so backward it'd take me that long to get on line.

"Believe me after a while you won't want to bother with it much at all, apart from research."

"There's no phone signal here. How can I keep in touch with civilization?"

"This is civilization. What you think of as civilization is simply vulgar trash designed to keep the masses happy."

"Half an hour?" I repeated.

"No longer. There's WiFi all over the house so you can use your laptop anywhere but I can check how long you've been on for and where you've been." So she'd be spying on me. "And speaking of plenty to read," she continued, "I must just nip and get something."

She left the room and it was suddenly quiet. I know that sounds silly but to be in the room without her talking at me was such a change that the sudden quiet really struck me. Through the window I saw that the sky was already darker than when I'd first arrived and I could see what she meant about the light. The sides of the hills weren't green any more, they were almost purple and the tops of the hills looked very dark. I could imagine what it would be like to be on one of those hills, unable to find your way down in the dark. Just looking through the window gave me a sense this place was not quite what it seemed.

"Here we are," she said as she breezed back in and handed me a sheet of paper.

"What's this?" I asked.

"Your reading list. I can't hope to develop your maths or sciences while you're here but English, Art and History I can help you with and here's where we start. I want you to have read at least half the books on this list by the time you start school in September."

"But we don't even know which school I'll be going to in September," I reminded her. "They might not need me to have read any of these!"

"I need you to have read these," she said with a strong emphasis on the 'I'.

I scanned the list quickly and recognised some of the titles. "I'm reading 'Catcher in the Rye' at the moment!" I said, thinking she might be pleased I was reading one of them but all she said was, "Good. Try to finish it by the end of the week. It's not long, and I want you to have read the one at the top of the list by the end of next week because it's the next one up at the book club so we can talk about it beforehand."

"What?" My heart sank at the thoughts. "You're taking me to a book club?"

She almost laughed. "A bunch of middle aged women nattering about a book over coffee and sandwiches? Even I'm not that cruel, but it would be useful to have someone to talk it over with before we meet up. Some of them think they're so clever when really they're just pretentious."

"Sounds like fun," I said.

'I'm not sure I enjoy it that much myself, but it's a way of keeping abreast of things."

"You mean gossip," I suggested and she nodded.

"Mind you," she sounded as if she'd suddenly had a great idea. "If you were to break any of my rules it would be a suitable punishment …"

"Oh, no, please…" I pleaded.

"Or if not to attend the book club perhaps to provide the sandwiches…" She was toying with me.

"No good at sandwiches, I'm afraid. Whenever I make a sandwich all the contents leap out as I lift it towards my mouth. It's as if they're still alive and making a final bid for freedom."

"Then you can bake a cake," she suggested, and I knew she probably wasn't serious but I still felt the need to head it off.

"Oh, no," I said. "No – no – no – no – no. Absolutely not. I can't cook. I've tried, and failed. I don't know why. My Home Economics teacher says I'm the worst pupil she's ever had. And believe me, she's old, so she's had a lot of them. Sorry. Just can't."

She looked at me for a moment and then asked, "How old are you, child?"

"Fifteen," I replied. "You know that. Oh, and thanks for the card and cheque, by the way."

"The thanks is a little late, but appreciated nevertheless. A short note would have been better, however busy you might have been. Good manners are important, they help build character." I was beginning to squirm. If this was a point scoring exercise she was winning hands down and I knew she was right. And she hadn't finished.

"The reason I ask about your age is, you're still young. You really do have most of your life in front of you and it's far too early to start saying you can't do things just because you haven't given it a proper go or you assume you won't like it." I wanted to point out that we'd gone from cakes and sandwiches to the meaning of life in one jump and it really wasn't that big a deal, but I knew there was no point in arguing. And anyway, she was probably right. And then the tone of her voice changed again and she said, "Now, unpack and have a shower. Supper will be ready in an hour and if you can keep a civil tongue in your head I might even let you have a glass of wine."

When I got downstairs Uncle Frank was opening a bottle of red wine.

"Aha! Here she is, the girl of the hour," he smiled as he poured me a glass and we chatted while Joan set the table. Supper was roast lamb. "This is delicious!" I said and it wasn't the wine talking, it really was good. I hadn't realised how hungry I was until I sat down but then I remembered all I'd eaten since breakfast were some sandwiches and biscuits I bought with the money Miss Kimble gave me.

"Thank you very much," said Frank. "You can come again."

"Did you do this?" I asked.

"Of course! I do most of the cooking around here."

"It's really soft and pink and tasty," I said.

"It's not bad," he admitted, "but actually I prefer hogget."

"What's that?" I asked.

"Basically older lamb. It has a stronger flavour but it's not so easy to get hold of these days."

"How come?" I asked.

"Well it's bigger than lamb and heavier to carry. At my age I can only carry one lamb at a time and when I do get my hands on one the others bleat so loud I have to be quick in case the farmer hears and catches me at it."

I know I can be a bit slow at times, and this was one of them. It was only when I noticed them quietly giggling that I caught on.

"Are you telling me you nicked this?" I asked.

"Have you seen the price of a rack of lamb in the shops?" he asked. "I'm not paying that when they're almost right outside the back door just asking to be taken!"

"It's well known that food tastes better when you haven't paid for it," Joan chipped in with a wink.

"The food at school was awful," I pointed out, "and it turns out my dad hadn't paid for it, so there goes that theory!"

"If you think this is good wait 'til you taste the food at the hotel," Frank said. "Perry's a genius!"

"Who's Perry?" I asked.

"An absolute Godsend," Joan replied. "He and Terry pretty much run the hotel for us. They're a great team. Perry's in charge of the cooking and Terry takes care of front of house, everything the guests actually see. You'll meet them tomorrow."

"Everyone wants to meet you," Frank said. "Your Grandmother's made you quite famous in the neighbourhood. She's busy tomorrow so I'll take you round to meet everyone."

I really didn't fancy the idea of being paraded all over the Lake District like some freak for the benefit of my Grandmother, but I realised it had to be done and it might not be so bad if it was with Frank.

It was strange being with the two of them. In some ways they were like an old couple who'd been married for ages and got on each other's nerves, but in other ways they were like a couple of kids, joking and laughing as if they had their own secret language. They were obviously making an effort to make me feel at home with all the usual questions about school and stuff, but at other times I had no idea who or what they were talking about and had the vague impression that they didn't want me to know either. Then again, that's normal for someone of my age when sitting at a table with so called 'grown ups'.

After I'd had enough to eat I realised how tired I was. I made my apologies and went up to my room. After I'd got into bed Joan came up to wish me goodnight. "I'm just doing this tonight to check you're settling in – don't think I'm going to get into the habit of telling you bed time stories," she said.

"You probably wouldn't like the kind of stories I like to hear late at night," I told her. She raised an eyebrow in a way that was by then becoming familiar. "Haunted houses, vanishing hitch hikers, blood dripping on car roofs, all that sort of stuff," I said and she laughed.

"My dear girl I've been in more haunted houses and scary situations than you've had hot dinners – it's one of the many perks of being older. But don't worry: the scariest thing in this house is me, and you've made a good start in conquering your fear." And with that she bent down to kiss me on the forehead (which took me by surprise), wished me goodnight and left me on my own.

As soon as I turned the bedside lamp off and rolled over to go to sleep everything that I'd shoved to the back of my mind came out to the front. I found myself going over everything that had happened that day, starting with the fight in the morning. All that and now here I was, alone in a room I'd not seen since I was a kid. And when I let that thought into my head I started to feel like a kid again, a little kid who was very much alone and suddenly lonely and worried about things. I was here because I had nowhere else to go, no one else wanted me. School didn't want me anymore and even my parents had disappeared. I realised I wasn't worried about them any more, I was angry with them for dumping all this on me. It wasn't fair. I pulled the duvet tighter round me and quietly cried myself to sleep.

5

I'd forgotten to set my alarm so by the time I woke up Joan had gone to the hotel and Frank was in the living room reading the paper. I could smell breakfast and as I walked downstairs he leaped into action and in no time I was sitting across the table from a beaming bald bloke knocking back probably his thirty fifth coffee of the morning. This was how I always remembered him, and he hadn't changed.

But his car had.

"There isn't room to open both doors so you'll have to wait here for a moment," he said as he lifted the door to the garage. Seconds later an engine roared into life and out came an old, bright red Porsche 911. And I mean old. Not classic motor worth a mint old, but not rust bucket falling apart old either. It just looked as if it had seen better days.

He got out again to close the garage door and then came round to the passenger side to open the door for me. "You're such a gentleman, thank you kind sir!" I said as I got in. The seats weren't even leather, they were a kind of knitted black fabric with what looked like 'leatherette' bits at the side. The sort of thing your gran would knit. (Well, not my gran, obviously, but someone else's gran. A normal gran.)

"This is a bit old," I teased him as he got back in.

"So am I," he said.

"And it's a bit red." It was too early in the morning for me to look at the bright bonnet through the windscreen.

"Best colour for around here," he said as he put it into gear and sped off. "If you get stuck in a snowdrift the rescue team can spot you more easily."

"That's reassuring," I nodded. I knew he was joking, but I wasn't sure how much. And then I noticed, "You haven't even got a CD player, this thing takes cassettes!"

"There's a box of cassettes behind you if you want to choose the music," he nodded over his shoulder. It was mostly classical and I wasn't in the mood so I didn't.

We drove up and down hills and onto wide open empty roads and busy dual carriageways, stopping at lay-bys so I could look at particular views, and stopping at shops and houses so that I could be introduced to people. Or shown off to them, I'm not sure which, really. But everyone was nice, everyone knew what Joan could be like but was obviously still fond of her, and I didn't feel much like a freak show exhibit after all.

We got to the hotel for a late lunch. Joan was sitting at a table for three when we arrived and as soon as we sat down a good looking young man in a rather nice suit appeared with some menus.

"Thanks, Terry," Joan said as she took hers. "This is Camille."

He handed me a menu and then stood looking at me with his head cocked to one side for a moment, which was rather disconcerting. "Well," he said finally, "you don't look like a fugitive juvenile delinquent who's likely to scarper before paying the bill but, as in all things, I'll take Joan's word for it. I'll get the wine."

"Don't mind him," Frank winked at me as he walked away. "He makes his mind up as soon as he sees someone if he's going to like them or not, and that's his way of saying he likes you."

My dad would have said he was a 'bottle of coffee' (apparently you used to be able to buy coffee in bottles and it was called 'Camp Coffee') and I suddenly missed my dad. He'd have loved it here.

Well, maybe without Joan.

After lunch, which was as good as Frank said it

would be, we left Joan at the hotel and drove to yet another small town / large village – I still can't tell the difference – and a strangely old fashioned shop where I got kitted out for walking with boots, socks, jacket, fleeces, you name it. On the way back to Joan's I was wondering why he'd taken me there when there were plenty of similar but more modern shops much closer by.

Then something occurred to me.

"Er, Frank, I know you were joking about the lamb last night – "

"Who says I was joking?" he asked.

"But seriously, have we just shop lifted all that outdoors clothing?"

"Course we haven't, you stupid girl! What do you take me for?"

"Well when did you pay for it? I didn't see you."

"Oh, God," he sighed, "spot the city kid. We don't actually pay for stuff here, we just keep a tab on who owes what and it all comes out in the wash at some point."

"How do you mean?"

"Well, for example, I have a couple of friends, Jock and Henry. Both farmers, as it happens. Miles apart they live, other ends of the county. A couple of years ago Jock needed a new telly and I knew that Henry had some over at his farm."

"Why would he have televisions if he's a farmer?"

"Some useful advice for life, girl: don't ask, just listen. So I took Jock over to meet Henry, not knowing that they already knew each other and that Jock owed Henry some money. Henry said Jock couldn't have a telly until he'd paid back at least some of what he owed him. With me so far?"

"I think so, yes," I said, but I was beginning to wonder.

"So I paid Henry some of what Jock owed him, so Jock owed me instead, at which point everyone was happy and Jock got his new telly. Then the next time I was over at Jock's he took me to one of his barns and, lo and behold, under a pile of hay stacks and sheets was this little beauty which had just been sitting there quietly for a few years. So I took this in exchange for what he owed both me and Henry and then I paid Henry the rest of what Jock owed him."

When people in this part of the country are talking about something a bit unusual or odd they say it's a 'bit of a rum do'. I got the impression Frank's car was a bit of a rum do so I didn't ask any more. It's a nice car, though. For an old one. Then again, Frank's not too bad, for an old one.

But then there was another 'rum do' when we got home that afternoon. Miss Kimble phoned at tea time and told me a couple of guys in dark suits had come looking for me.

"What for?" I asked.

"They said they wanted to talk to you about your dad."

"What about?"

"Well that's the thing. The Head asked them what it was all about and they wouldn't tell her so she sent them packing. What worries me is she doesn't think it's anything to do with the school, since you're no longer under our care, so she hasn't told the Police, which I think she ought to have done. I only heard about it from the Receptionist so I thought I'd better let you know."

I don't know whether it was fear or common sense that kicked in but at that point I passed Miss K over to Joan, who was furious by the time she finished the call. "I find it extraordinary that your half baked idiot of a Headmistress didn't think to contact the Police about this, and I think Miss Kimble should have spoken straight to me."

"Don't blame her," I said, "The Beak will be furious if she finds out Miss K's gone behind her back."

"I got that impression while I was talking to her, poor girl. Still, she did the right thing. In view of the fact that we can't contact either of your parents it is, to say the least, rather odd that two chaps should turn up wanting to talk to you about your father."

"There's probably some perfectly innocent explanation," I said, as much to reassure myself as her, but she shook her head.

"Your father is negligent, unreliable, and a fantasist who always thinks that whatever he's involved in at the moment is the one really big deal he needs so that you can all live happily ever after, but this is in an altogether different league. He would never involve you or your mother or risk your safety in any way. This is more serious that your idiot Headmistress realises, or cares to. Your father's obviously got himself into something really stupid this time." She looked deep in thought for a moment and then said, "I need to talk to Harry," and took the phone into another room.

"Who's Harry?" I asked Frank.

"Detective Inspector Harry Wheatman," Frank explained. "Old friend of hers. He'll either put her mind at rest or do something about it."

"Does she know absolutely everyone around here?" I asked, to which he smiled and said "She knows everyone and everything that matters around here. Or, to put it another way, anyone or anything she doesn't know doesn't really matter." He paused, and then added, "At least not to her."

She was gone a long time and came back with quite a serious expression on her face. "Harry is of a mind to have your parents officially recorded as 'Missing Persons' if we don't hear from them within the next forty eight hours," she said. That made my heart leap because it suddenly seemed serious. It hadn't even occurred to me that something bad might have happened to them, and now suddenly we were talking about them being officially classed as missing. But then she said, "I pointed out that, knowing your father, the likelihood is they've skipped the country in order to avoid people he owes money to and will turn up safe and sound when the situation's resolved or at least the pressure's off. We decided to talk about it again in a couple of days. He's actually more concerned about strange men turning up at boarding schools asking to talk to girls and he's doing something about that right now." She smiled and said, "I take it you don't like your former Headmistress?"

"I don't think anyone does, did, or ever will," I said.

"Then you'll be pleased to know she's going to get a bit of a rollicking for this. And don't worry, I mentioned how sensible and helpful Miss Kimble had been and he'll pass that on to the officers who pay your old school a little visit."

For the rest of the evening I was quietly pleased at the thoughts of The Beak getting a visit from the police, so went to bed in quite a good mood, but that night I had all sorts of strange dreams about my parents and in the morning I woke up more concerned about them than ever. I told Joan how worried I was because my dad could go weeks without even texting me but my mum usually phoned me a couple of times a week.

"Apart from the men in dark suits we've been here before," she said. "I wouldn't worry about it. You're safe here and your parents will turn up sooner or later and all will be well once more. At least until the next time." I knew she was trying to reassure me but she didn't quite succeed. The mention of the men in dark suits told me she was as worried as I was, and we both knew there was nothing we could do.

And that made me feel worse.

6

After I'd been there for a few days I'd met most of the people who lived in the village or worked at the hotel and they all seemed friendly, so I was past the stage where I felt like some kind of freak being shown off to everyone.

I was on my own for most of the day, with Joan and Frank usually at the hotel, and I settled in to a routine. I finished 'The Catcher in the Rye' and started working my way through the other books on the list. I would read for a while in the mornings after they'd gone and again later in the day, and then the rest of the morning would be taken up with drawing and making myself some lunch if they weren't around. There were also a few little jobs Joan would ask me to do, like load and unload the dishwasher and the washing machine, which I didn't mind. The threat of working at the hotel never really came to much.

The only person I didn't like was Geraldine, the chambermaid from the hotel who came over to do an hour or two's cleaning at the house in the afternoons. The first time I saw her she just grunted and looked disappointed, as if I'd promised to bring her something and then forgot. I'd never met her before and even before we spoke I could tell she didn't like me, which made me not like her.

So on days when I was on my own I'd go for a walk in the afternoon – after leaving a message about where I was going and how long I'd be – so that I wouldn't be there when she was. I know that sounds pathetic, but there you go. Anyway I didn't mind because the strange thing was I really got into the whole walking over the countryside around the lake and through the village type of thing. It was good to be doing something physical, and something which seemed to help me think and at the same time clear my mind. Some of the fells were quite steep so there'd be times when I'd be working really hard just getting to the top of a hill but then when I got to the top and looked down the views were amazing and definitely worth the effort. So many different shapes, shades and colours, and within a day or two I noticed that each day the same scenery would be different, sometimes completely different. It seemed as if the light in the sky, the light reflected on the water of the lake, the colours of the hills and fells all around, even the air itself, all combined in different ways to produce different effects, and I found myself looking forward to seeing what it all looked like each day.

And another odd thing: for the first few days I tried frantically to contact my friends whenever I got the chance, but because they were in school when I could get a signal I could only leave messages, and when they were out of school and could phone me at the house I was with Joan and Frank, and sometimes other people as well, and it was a bit awkward. And I know this sounds strange, but I liked being with Joan and Frank and didn't really want to be interrupted. So after a week or so I stopped bothering, and so did they. I had a vague idea about asking one or two of them to come up and stay over the summer, but thought I'd better leave it until I knew for sure what was happening with my mum and dad and everything, and the longer I left it the less sure I was that I wanted them to come anyway. This was a new life now, different from my old one, and I was getting used to it. I'd be at a new school in September and at that point I'd be able to get back in touch with my old friends and at the same time make new ones.

After two weeks I was getting to know the area quite well, so one day I went for a longer walk. I looked at the map and worked out roughly where

I was going and where I'd end up before having to come home, but then I forgot to take the map with me and got ever so slightly confused. Not lost, you understand, just a bit confused about where things were in relation to each other. Which is totally different from being lost. Being lost is when you have absolutely no idea where the hell you are and no chance of finding your way back. I knew roughly where I was, it was just that things weren't where I'd been expecting them to be. But I wasn't lost.

And even if I had been lost I wasn't lost for very long because when I came round the other side of the hill I was walking down I could see a narrow winding road that passed through the valley between the bottom of the hill I was on and another one opposite. You're never really lost if you can see a road.

At the bottom of the hill on the opposite side was a bus shelter. A grey bus shelter made from the same lakeland slate Joan's house was made from and obviously designed to withstand the worst of the weather. It looked like a mini shepherd's hut with one side open to the world, but instead of a shepherd inside it there looked to be a witch. Someone sitting on the bench in the shelter dressed all in black. Not a witch, I realised as I got towards the bottom of the hill and could see more clearly, more like a Goth. A Goth in a bus shelter. In darkest Cumbria.

"All right?" she called across the road as I reached the bottom of the hill.

"All right?" I called back and crossed over to her. I don't really know why I walked over to her because it wasn't the way I needed to go – at least I thought it wasn't – I suppose she seemed friendly and it would have been rude not to.

I'm glad I did.

"Can I ask a favour?" she said as I reached the bus stop.

"What?"

"Can I borrow your phone for a minute?"

"I doubt you'll get a signal," I said as I handed it over.

"What network are you on?" she asked as she looked at the screen and then said "Oh, that'll work. Come with me a minute." Instantly she was about ten paces ahead of me going up the hill behind the shelter. "You get a signal about half way up here but then you lose it if you go right to the top 'cos it bounces off this hill onto that one," she called over her shoulder. "Ah! Gotcha!" She tapped in a number as I caught up with her and a moment later said, "Dad, can you pick me up, please?" There was a brief pause and then she said, "The bus stop at the bottom of Kirkstile." By then I was close enough to hear her dad, not because the signal was good but because he was pretty loud.

"Why are you at the bus stop?" he was asking.

"I'm on my way home but the next bus isn't for an hour."

"Why are you on your way home?"

"I left school early."

"And why did you leave school early?"

"I got into trouble for my uniform." I laughed out loud and she gave me a quick dirty look before going on to say, "Well I'm not really wearing it, so Mr Hinchcliffe sent me to Mrs Wallasey and Mrs Wallasey sent me to Mr Adams and he was going to phone you so -" she paused while her dad said something and then she mumbled, "thanks, dad," ended the call and passed the phone back to me.

"So that's not your school uniform?" I asked, slightly sarcastically.

"It was, but they changed it last week to a blue gingham pinafore dress with a straw boater and I forgot." She was nearly as good as me, I thought. "So now I'm dead meat."

"It can't be that bad," I said.

"It is," she replied. "It really is that bad. Mrs Wallasey – that's my head of year – will already have phoned my mum and Mr Adams – he's the head – will phone my dad 'cos they're both in the Rotary club so my mum and dad will get their ears bent in stereo, which means they'll bend my ears in stereo and all because just for once I turned up at school in what I wanted to wear instead of what they told me to wear because I'm SICK!" she shouted up the hill. "I'm sick of this boring school and this boring village and this boring life!"

"I love it here!" I said, as much as anything to lighten the mood.

"That's 'cos you don't live here," she replied. "You can stay as long as you like but you're free to go home whenever."

Actually, I'm not, I thought. But I didn't say anything.

"I can't escape," she continued. "This is home. I'm not free to go anywhere. Even the journey from school involves two clapped out bone shaking pre-war buses. That's why I'm here now. I left school an hour ago and I'm not even half way home yet."

"Does it always take that long?" I asked.

"Only when you bunk off," she smiled. "School lays on a coach for all the little automatons to be shuffled in and out at the right time like the good little sheep we are." She looked up the hill again and shouted "I'm sick of being one of the good sheep! I'm sick of it! D'ya hear me?" The last few words were so loud that they reverberated off the hills slightly and the silence that followed clearly suggested no one had heard, or could hear, or cared less. She turned back to me and said, "You're Camille, aren't you?"

"How do you know?" I was genuinely surprised.

"You just might possibly have noticed that the most interesting thing people around here can find to talk about is other people. So when someone new arrives it gives them something else to talk about for a while. Something new and exciting. There probably wouldn't be much more excitement generated if Queen Catherine herself came to open the public loos in the village square."

"I didn't notice any loos in the village square."

"That's because there aren't any, but if they thought they could get her to come and open them they'd build some," she said. "I'm Sarah, by the way, and thanks for the phone."

"That's all right," I shrugged. "Glad I could help."

"What are you doing now?" she asked.

"I'm going back to my Grandmother's," I nodded down the road.

"You're lost," she said.

"No, I'm not."

"Where are you going?" she asked again.

"I told you. Back to my Grandmother's," and again I nodded down the road.

"You're lost," she repeated. "Your Grandmother's is that way," she nodded in the opposite direction. She might have been right but she might just have been winding me up and she saw the confusion on my face and laughed. "Honestly!" she said again. "It's that way!"

"I'd better be getting back, then," I said.

"You might as well stay with me," she said. "You'll only get lost again and there'll be no one else to point you in the right direction." I hesitated and she said, "Aw, go on, stay, please. My mum and dad know Joan and my dad'll give you a lift home and he won't have a go at me while you're with us and by the time we've dropped you off he'll have calmed down a bit so I'll only have my mum to deal with." She smiled sweetly and put her hands together. "Please..." she pleaded and when I nodded she said, "Thanks, mate – I owe you!"

We sat on the bench in the shelter to wait for her dad. "How long have you been a Goth?" I asked.

"Dunno, really," she shrugged. "Couple of years, on and off. It's not a full time thing."

"So you're a part time Goth?"

"I just like wearing different clothes depending on what mood I'm in. Today I'm in a Goth mood but that doesn't mean I'm a 'Goth'. I hate being labelled like that."

"I know what you mean."

"So what's it like living with The Godmother?"

"Huh?"

"Didn't you know? That's what they call Joan, at least behind her back. 'The Godmother', like a Godfather in the Mafia."

"I didn't know," I laughed, "but it suits her."

"Half the people around here think she's wonderful, the other half are scared to death of her."

"Which side are you on?" I asked.

"My parents think she's great as long as you don't get on the wrong side of her. I've only met her a couple of times. The important thing is: what do you think of her?"

"She takes a bit of getting used to," I said. "But I think I'm getting used to her."

The peace and quite was broken by the sound of an engine some way off. "Here he comes," she said. "And he's in the van. That means I've been a naughty girl. When he's in a good mood and I'm his little Princess he picks me up in the car. When he's in a bad mood it's the van."

"Is it all right my being here, really?" I asked.

"Yeah, 'course. You can sit between us." Just then a large Grey transit van pulled up. "You get in first," she said then opened the door. "Thanks, Dad," she called up. "Can we give Camille a lift back to Joan's? She has no idea where she is."

"Suppose so," he said but then smiled at me and said "I was wondering when we'd meet you. I'm Chris. Father of trouble," he nodded towards Sarah as she climbed in beside me and slammed the door shut. The van shot off up the road. After I'd said 'hello' I couldn't think of anything to say. The only thing I could think of was that – apart from a school mini bus which probably doesn't count – this was the first time I'd ever been in a van and it was funny being so high up and bouncing about without any seat belts, but I thought that might sound snotty so I kept quiet. And keeping quiet meant I noticed the atmosphere.

"Been busy?" Sarah asked, eventually.

"I was in the middle of something when you phoned, since you ask," Chris said.

"What do you do?" I asked, being polite.

"He's a master craftsman," Sarah said before he could. "He restores old buildings and old furniture, makes new furniture, upholstery, interior design, all that sort of stuff."

"Her mother does most of the interior design," he said.

"She's not as good as he is, though," she winked at me.

"And you don't get round me as easily as that," he said.

"I'm not trying to," she said with a slight whine, which made it clear she was.

"I'm the craftsman," he said to me and then nodded to her. "She's story teller."

"That's not true!" she said. "That's Duncan." I looked at her and she explained, "My brother. He's a journalist. Absolutely full of horse manure, as they all are."

"At least he's got a career," her dad said. "God knows what you're going to do for a living." I could see why she wanted me there, sitting between them. I was looking from one to the other as if they were in a tennis match and it felt ridiculous, but just to look straight ahead when all this was going on would have seemed rude.

"So what are you working on?" she asked.

"If you ever paid the slightest attention to anything I said at home you'd know."

"I do, Daddy, but you have so many talents and you're in such demand it's sometimes difficult to keep track."

"See what I mean?" he asked me. "Do you treat your dad like this?"

"Don't really get the chance," I said, but then thought actually yes, I do, when I get the chance. I just wished I got the chance more often. I wished I had the chance right then. I wished I knew where on earth he was right then.

"Do you want to come for tea tomorrow?" Sarah asked.

"Yeah, that'd be great, thanks. What time?"

"When can you make it? I'll be home alone and bored out of my brain all day."

"You'll be at school, so you won't be home until four thirty," her dad said.

"Nope," she said flatly. "Adams is phoning you tonight. He's suspending me."

"No he isn't."

"Yes he is."

"No he isn't, he's already phoned me."

"What?"

"And it's mister Adams to you."

"Oh really, that is so unfair! The least I was hoping for was a couple of days off!"

"Which is exactly why he's not suspending you."

"Yeah, but I'm bored. I need a break from school."

"It's a few weeks to the end of term and then

almost as soon as you go back you're on study leave," he pointed out. "And anyway you've just told Camille you'd be home alone tomorrow 'bored out of your brain' all day. You don't want to be 'bored out of your brain', do you?" He had her, and she knew it.

"You see?" she said to me. "This place is like a prison, but more subtle. You can go anywhere you like, do anything you like, you just can't get away and you can't get away with anything. Better make it five o'clock, then."

"I don't even know where you live," I pointed out.

"If Joan or Frank can't drop you off we'll pick you up," she said. "Phone me to let me know which it is."

"I haven't got your number."

"You have, I put it into your contacts while I was borrowing your phone."

"She's like that," her dad said. "Sly."

She reached across me and thumped him and I knew they were all right.

She must have been right about me having no idea where I was because I was quite surprised when the van turned a corner and I realised we were on the road which ran alongside the lake. A moment later I could see Joan's house. I had no idea how we'd got there. I'm still not sure, to be honest.

The van pulled up outside the gate. "Say Hi to Joan and Frank," Chris said, "and we'll see you tomorrow. Nice meeting you." Sarah jumped down to let me out and mouthed 'thank you' to me as she climbed back into the van.

"Thanks for the lift," I called as she closed the door and the van drove off. By the time I'd reached the front door Joan was standing in the doorway.

"Was that Chris Mackie's Van?" she asked.

"Yeah, I met Sarah and he picked us up from the bus stop. He says Hi."

"He should," she grunted. "He owes me money."

"I thought you didn't use money around here," I said.

"Frank might not. I do."

7

In the end I decided to walk to Sarah's. When I looked at the map I realised it wasn't much further than my usual walk but it would be a different route, which would be interesting. The only problem was it meant I left the house later than usual so I had to put up with Geraldine crashing the hoover into the walls and the furniture, which I'm sure she was doing deliberately to express her irritation at me being there. I still wasn't sure what I'd done to offend her so I decided it was a territorial thing, and all the noise she was making was like a cat spraying on the furniture.

Then she started leaving the radio on in every room she went into while I was trying to finish the book I was reading. I put up with it for as long as I could but then went to ask her to switch them off but couldn't find her, so I went round the house switching them off one by one. She walked into the dining room just as I was about to turn that one off and she looked at me as if I'd been caught eating food from out of the bin.

Sarah's house was a mile or so behind the hills

on the other side of the lake from Joan's, so I had to begin by walking half way around the lake. I did think – briefly – about using the boat. It would have saved a lot of time and effort but by then I knew that if Joan said don't do something it really was best not to do it. Even so, I felt a bit annoyed with myself as I walked past the boat house. If it had been at school and we'd been told not to use it I'd have done so just to spite them, so what was different here? Was it fear of Joan? Maybe. She could be scarier than The Beak, but there was more to it than that. I had to admit to myself that I didn't want to upset her. Did that mean I was becoming a nicer person? Maybe. Or was I just getting soft? Ugh. Hope not.

Then I remembered I didn't know anything about boats or outboard motors and I didn't know how to row. I'd only ever tried it once in my entire life, when I was with my dad on a boating lake somewhere years ago, and I was rubbish.

So that was that. I walked.

Even though it was a glorious spring day there was hardly anyone in sight, just a couple having a picnic on the far side of the lake and apart from that there was no one. Joan and Frank said this was the quiet end of the Lake District where people didn't go much and they were right.

The edge of the island was all rocks and shingle, with a huge sign saying

Private Property
Dangerous terrain
Trespassers will be prosecuted

to warn people off, and beyond that just trees and overgrowth. I thought I saw something moving into the overgrowth so I stood and watched for a minute but didn't see anything else. Maybe I'd just imagined it.

I kept glancing over to the island to see if there was anything there and so I wasn't really looking where I was going. I suddenly stumbled over a rock or something and instinctively put my hands out in front of me as I fell and landed in some thistles. I rolled over and down the hill a couple of times and came to a halt. My hands were stinging like hell and I know it's stupid but I suddenly wanted to cry. Sitting there with stinging hands suddenly made me feel really alone and sorry for myself.

I remembered being out with my mum once somewhere when I was little and tripping over a kerb stone. I grazed my knee, burst into tears and had to be carried all the way home. She was cross at having to carry me and said it was my own fault for not looking where I was going. Now, all those years later, I felt as if I was still a stupid kid doing the same stupid thing again. I took a couple of deep breaths to fight back the tears and then slowly and carefully stood up. When I knew I was okay and could still walk I breathed a sigh of relief and silently thanked the Gods I hadn't twisted my ankle. That would have been really bad. I'd have had to crawl on my hands and knees all the way back to the house. Geraldine would have loved that and Joan would know for sure I was an idiot. I didn't know which would be worse.

I walked on briskly, making sure I was watching where I was going and trying to forget about the stinging on my hands, when I had an idea. I walked down to the edge of the lake and squatted down to put my hands in the water. It was icy cold and helped to numb the pain for a while until I couldn't keep my hands in there any longer.

I stood up and shook my hands dry and was about to turn back to the path when I noticed movement on the island and this time I knew I wasn't mistaken. I caught a glimpse of something brown and low down on four legs. It was walking along the edge of the island but almost as soon as I saw it whatever it was disappeared further inland into the overgrowth. It could almost have been a bear walking on all fours but it wasn't furry enough. I stood watching for a couple of minutes but didn't see it again.

I walked the rest of the way carefully, looking where I was going all the time and wishing I'd taken Frank up on the offer of a couple of walking sticks when he was kitting me out. At the time I laughed them off as something only old people needed but now I realised how useful they could be.

All the way over to Sarah's I was trying to work out what it was I'd seen. It might have been a seal. It had that kind of belly flop movement seals have on dry land. But it wasn't low down enough to be a seal, it looked to be walking on all fours. That's why I thought of a bear when I first saw it.

I stopped and stared again for a few moments, hoping to see it again but of course I didn't, and the longer I looked hopefully towards the island the less sure I was of exactly what it was I'd seen. Perhaps it was a small-ish bear that had come out of the water with its fur all wet against its body. But surely Joan or Frank would have mentioned if the island had bears, wouldn't they?

Sarah's house was smaller than Joan's but had a bigger garden that went all around the house and her dad ran his business from a huge workshop at the side of the house. Before we ate

Sarah and I hung out in her room for a while and she told me Denise, her mum, had spent most of the day preparing the meal and the tablecloth was only used for special occasions. "So please," she said, "do something awful. Behave obnoxiously. Belch and fart your way through the main course. Vomit over dessert or something – anything – because if you're as nice and well behaved as they expect you to be I'll never hear the last of it!"

"If I do any of that I'll never hear the last of it – from my Grandmother!"

"How is the Godmother?" she laughed. "I think my dad's a bit scared of her."

"I think he owes her some money," I whispered.

"He owes everybody money," she said.

"Bit like my dad, then."

"See? We have so much in common! I knew we were going to get on!"

The meal was delicious but I had no idea what I was eating and it felt awkward to ask because I think I was supposed to know, so I just kept saying how lovely it was, which made Denise smile and Sarah kick me under the table. Half way through the main course the front door opened and a voice called out "Anyone home?"

Denise leapt to her feet with a squeal of delight and ran to the hall while Sarah groaned and said,

"Just what we need, the return of the prodigal son."

"Since we have a guest this evening," Chris said, "would it kill you to be welcoming to your brother, just for once?" He got up from the table and went out to the hall.

"What's wrong with your brother?" I asked.

"He's a complete and total lanyard," she said.

"A what?"

"A lanyard. You know, those ID badges people have to wear around their necks at work? That's what he is – lightweight, demeaning, worthless, but still a weight around your neck."

I just assumed it was normal sibling hatred. He seemed charming to me.

"Hello," he held out his hand as he walked into the kitchen. "I'm Duncan. You must be Camille." We shook hands as he said, "I've heard a lot about you."

"All good, I hope!" I smiled at him and could have kicked myself. What a stupid thing to say! It just came out, but I knew it would sound like I was fishing for compliments and I knew the fun Sarah would have with it. I could feel myself starting to get all hot in the face, and when he politely turned away I knew he was literally trying to save my blushes.

Sarah came to the rescue. "He's only being nice to you because he thinks you're rich," she said. "I told him you were a child movie star who'd used her millions to set herself up as an international money launderer," and with that from her and a shrug from him the awkwardness was over. For a while.

He took his stuff upstairs and by the time he came back a place had been laid for him at the table, right opposite me.

"So what are you doing here?" Sarah asked. "Did you get the boot?"

"I've got tomorrow off so I thought I'd come and spend it in the warm and welcoming bosom of my family," he beamed around the table.

"You mean you thought you'd scrounge a free meal and get mum to do your washing," Sarah grunted.

"Don't start," Chris warned her. There was a second's awkward silence which was broken by Duncan asking about how I liked it round here, and how Joan and Frank were, and he seemed genuinely interested and interesting. Out of the corner of my eye I caught Sarah pulling faces and I wasn't sure if they were at me or at him, but either way I thought she was just attention seeking so I ignored her and carried on with the conversation.

"So you're a journalist?" I asked. Stupid question, I know, 'cos I already knew that but he might not have known I knew and you have to start somewhere.

"Trainee," he said. "I'm one of the last of my breed, someone who goes straight from school to work for a local paper learning the job as I go. Nowadays most journalists go to university, spend three years drinking and clubbing -"

"Sounds good to me!" Sarah interrupted.

"It would," he said without missing a beat and then continued, "then they work like hell for the last couple of months, get their degree and then go on to do a post grad in journalism and after all that they end up no further than where I am now, but with a massive student loan to pay back."

"Except they're on the national dailies covering the big events of the day," Sarah said, "while you're stuck on some small town rag covering the local primary school's production of 'Aladdin'." She got up to refill the water jug.

"Actually they're stuck at a desk doing boring stuff on a computer that a robot could do," he called after her. "Most of them will never get much further. At least this way I'm out in the field getting real stories for myself and that's how you find the big story that makes your career."

"Yup," she said to me as she plonked the jug back on the table. "He's certainly 'out in the field' – every time a cow gives birth within a fifty mile radius he's out there in the field covering it for the front page, and covering himself in cow dung."

"This is developing into one of those evenings, I fear," Chris said as he topped up Denise's wine glass and then his own. "In which case I'm going to sit in the garden. You coming?" Denise nodded and they both stood up.

"Sorry about this, Camille," Denise said, "but welcome to our world." She smiled rather sadly as she raised her glass in a toast to me and they went out into the garden.

"You have to spoil everything, don't you?" Duncan said when they'd gone.

"You started it," Sarah said.

"How did I start it?"

"You came home."

He sighed in irritation and turned back to me. "I'm assuming you've been warned about my sister," he said.

"Not really," I said, "but I'm learning." She pulled a face at me. "So is that your plan, to find the big story that makes your reputation?" I asked.

"Absolutely. Break a good story and that's your chance to hit the big time and get a name for yourself. Meanwhile I'm honing my craft as I go and getting paid for it."

"I thought journalists started out writing blogs these days," I said.

"That's the problem with blogs – anyone can have one, everyone's got one and most of them aren't worth reading because they're either so dull or badly written. Most bloggers really ought to stick to diaries and keep their thoughts to themselves – no one else is that interested."

"A bit harsh," I suggested.

"Life's tough," he shrugged.

"Oh he knows all about being tough," Sarah said. "You should have seen him first time he got dumped by a girl. Nicky Cadman, the school's resident hair flicking blonde. He bawled his eyes out for three days."

"For God's sake, Sarah, can you possibly cope, just for once, with not being the centre of everyone's attention? I'm trying to have an intelligent conversation here." For a split second I saw hurt on her face – or it might have been jealousy. She looked as if she was about to say something but instead just got up and walked out, slamming the door behind her.

There was another awkward silence and then he said, "I'm really sorry. I don't know what gets into her sometimes. She's a great kid in many ways and I love her loads, but she's her own worst enemy. It's almost as if she needs to mess things up to prove she's here, as if we wouldn't notice her if she behaved normally. Stick around here long enough and you'll get used to it. I notice it more now because I'm away."

"Maybe it's because you go away that she does it more when you come back," I suggested. "Her way of telling you she's missed you."

"If she behaves like that to everyone she's fond of she'll end up without any friends anywhere."

He was right, so we left it there and talked about other stuff. He asked about school and it seemed so far away by then, and so different from the school he'd been to. We found we had quite a bit in common – we both loved Art, English and History and pretty much hated everything else.

"PE teachers are the worst," he said.

I snorted, and realised the wine was beginning to get to me slightly. "They're harmless enough," I said.

"No they're not – they're all psychopaths!" he said and I began to giggle, I wasn't sure why. "They go on and on about how it's not the winning that matters, it's the taking part. So you take part, you don't win and then they play hell at you 'cos you didn't win!"

I laughed out loud at that – it is true after all – and by then he was well into his stride. "And then they get you standing out in a field in the freezing cold 'cos they think it's going to toughen you up, and you come back next lesson with a note from your mum asking to be excused games. 'Why can't you do games?' they ask, and you say it's 'cos you've got a cold. 'Why've you got a cold?' they ask, completely ignoring the fact that they made you stand in the freezing cold for an hour!'"

"Ah, you see! You're lucky!" I said. "At boarding school you can't bring a note from home even if you do have a stinking cold."

"Don't they have a matron or sick bay or something?"

"Oh, yeah, but you have to be dying of legionnaire's disease or something before they'll even give you an aspirin, let alone allow you into the sick bay. The nun who ran the sick bay at my school used to work in a laboratory but got chucked out for cruelty to the animals, so she became a nun so she could be cruel to kids instead."

After a while the conversation sort of trailed off and we just sat quietly.

It was nice.

"How are you getting home?" he asked after a while.

"Frank's picking me up."

"What time?"

"He just said to phone him when I'm ready."

"Oh, let's not bother him. I'll take you home."
I was about to ask and he said, "Yes, I've got a car.
I'm not offering you a piggy back. It's an old
banger but it runs well."

"You've had a drink," I pointed out.

"If you look carefully you'll see I've actually had
about two sips of one glass of white wine so really
I should be okay. If I miss the turning for Joan's
house and we crash into the lake and drown you
can blame me."

"Hey, but at least you'll have a story," I smiled.

"Damn!" he said. "You've found me out!"

I phoned Frank, who said he was grateful to
Duncan because he fancied an early night, and so
we chatted about nothing much for a while. Denise
came in and cleared up a bit while Chris sat with us
and it was almost normal apart from the absence
of Sarah and the fact that no one mentioned her.

I was starting to feel a bit tired so suggested we
go, and while Duncan went to get his keys I thanked
Chris and Denise, who apologised for Sarah.

"Seriously, I wouldn't worry about it," I said.
"I've just left a boarding school where most of the
girls were much worse than her!"

As I walked out to the car I got a text from Sarah:

My brother is the Devil and you are under age.
Do not get involved.

I didn't know if she was being serious or just trying to make a joke to get me on her side, but either way I ignored it.

It was only when we joined a road which followed the lake towards Joan's that I thought to ask, "They haven't got bears on that island, have they?"

"I wouldn't have thought so," he said and I could tell from his voice that he thought it was funny. I felt a bit silly, but having started I knew I had to carry on so I told him what I'd seen on the way to their house. He listened carefully but said "I don't know much about the wildlife there at all, actually. Whatever is there must be fairly happy because I doubt anyone's been on that island for years. I've always thought it would be a great place for paint-balling but my dad reckons it's been abandoned for so long it'll be completely overgrown and would cost too much to sort it all out." He paused, and then said, "So no, I've no idea what small furry creatures might be there."

The way he said 'small furry creatures' confirmed my suspicions that he thought I was silly so I changed the subject until we got to Joan's. I thanked him as I was getting out of the car and he sort of patted me on the shoulder as he said goodnight and drove off. I watched the tail lights disappear up the road and then turned to look at the lake. It was dark and still, with the moonlight reflected on the water. The sky was so dark and everything was so quiet I could easily have believed I was the only living creature in the world.

8

For the next few days I took the same route on my walk and I'd meet up with Sarah. Sometimes she'd come to Joan's, sometimes I'd go to hers, or we'd go into the village and hang out for a while and then go our separate ways. I hate to admit this but when she talked about her day, even the stupid and irritating things and the stupid and irritating people, I actually missed school. Not specifically St. Dunstan's but any school. I missed the noise and bustle and the contact with people my own age and the laughs and even the stupid stuff. She couldn't believe it and said that not having to go to school meant I was the luckiest girl on earth and that she'd swap with me in a flash if she could. And of course she was right, she would have swapped if she could have, but I'm sure she'd very quickly have felt the same way I did.

"You're so lucky," she'd say. "You're free!"

"You'll be on study leave soon."

"Yeah, but then I'm supposed to be revising for my exams. You're free."

"Yeah? Free to do what?"

"Anything you want!"

"Yeah, but what? You're the one who goes on about how boring it is to actually live here," and so it went. Every day.

And then things got less dull.

I got home – well, Joan's house, which I'd started to call home – one afternoon about a week after I first met Sarah and was surprised to see Joan's car parked outside. It was early for her to be home and I sensed something was wrong. I ran up the path and as I walked through front door I could hear someone clattering about in the kitchen and Joan talking in the living room. I went into the living room to find Joan sitting on one sofa and sitting on the one opposite was my dear mother.

"Hello, darling," she smiled at me. "You look well."

I stood frozen in the doorway while about a dozen different emotions ran through me all at once. Relief, that she was still alive and apparently safe and well, obviously, but also annoyance that she hadn't been in touch when she seemed to be all right and hurt that I'd been left like a piece of luggage to be picked up by Joan and then a load of other things which meant that, again, I'm afraid I lost it a bit and yelled, "Where the hell have you been?"

"Sit down, darling," she patted the cushion next to her on the sofa, "and I'll try to explain. Mum says you've been really good."

"To hell with that!" I shouted, "where – have – you – been? And where's dad?" I know that probably wasn't the most intelligent reaction since she'd just said she was going to explain but by then the anger had trumped all my other emotions and I just felt like letting rip.

"Camille, don't speak to your mother like that," Joan said.

"She can't just suddenly turn up and act as if everything's hunky dory!"

"She hasn't. It isn't. Close the door, sit down and listen," she instructed me in her most Grandmotherly voice. I looked at each of them and saw from their faces how things were. Joan was almost angry, but controlling it. My mother looked frightened, but not of Joan. I closed the door behind me and sat on the chair between them. When I was settled and quiet my grandmother took a deep breath and then spoke calmly and clearly.

"It would appear the reason we haven't heard much from your parents recently is that your father has been arrested," she said. I almost laughed. My Dad? I mean, I know he's an idiot sometimes, but arrested?

"What for?" I asked.

"We're not exactly sure." my mum said. This was getting ridiculous.

"What do you mean, you're not sure?" I asked. "He's got a solicitor, hasn't he? Doesn't he know? Haven't you spoken to him?"

"Just wait a moment," my mother waved her hand in the air in a Slow – Down – Shut – Up – Just – Listen kind of gesture. She paused and said, "He's not been arrested in this country. Everything would be much simpler if he had been. He's in Nicaragua."

'What's he doing in Nicaragua?"

"He was out there trying to chase some kind of business deal." As she said that there was the slightest sigh of irritation from Joan. My mother gave her a quick glance but didn't say anything. Just as well. She didn't have a leg to stand on. "I've spoken to a man from the foreign office and they're being as helpful as they can. It seems your father has got himself involved with some not very nice people who would appear to have cheated him and left him looking responsible for what they've been up to, so he's the one who's been arrested."

This was getting just better and better.

My father was an idiot.

A mug.

A Patsy.

Like those kids at school who join in something

to become popular and end up taking the blame for everyone else when it all goes wrong because they haven't got the wit to see what's going to happen. Ugh, how cringe-worthy it was to think my dad's one of those poor suckers.

"So what happens next?" I asked.

"That's the problem," she said. "It seems the police in Nicaragua know he's not entirely guilty but they don't want to let him go until they've caught the people he was dealing with. They think if they give him bail he'll skip the country."

"Well he would, if he had any sense," I said and she nodded.

"And that's why they've set bail at half a million dollars."

"How much?" It seemed like a ridiculous amount of money, even for my dad.

"The equivalent in Nicaraguan Cordobas of half a million US dollars, which is a little less than half a million pounds."

"You're kidding! We haven't got that kind of money!" Then I asked, "Have we?"

"No, darling, we haven't. I think we might have had if this particular deal had come off, but obviously it didn't," she said.

"Yet another of your father's harebrained schemes," Joan said, unnecessarily. She'd obviously been itching to say something and just couldn't hold back any longer.

"Not helping," I pointed out to her, and it felt good to be the one telling a grown up off, for once.

"Sorry. You're quite right," she said.

"The only way I could raise that kind of money would be to sell the house," my mother continued, "but then we'd have nowhere to live." I don't know how – perhaps my grandmother flinched ever so slightly – but I knew then that the subject had been discussed before I got home and Joan had said something along the lines of my mother and I could move in if we absolutely had to, but no way was she going to put up with my dad.

"What about the Foreign Office?" I asked. "Can't they get him out?" They both shuffled slightly uncomfortably and again I could tell this had been discussed.

"I don't think they really want to," my mother said. "They're being helpful but they've suggested that if this isn't handled delicately it could turn into what they call a 'Diplomatic Incident'. That's why they've managed to keep it out of the papers so far, but I don't think they really want to get too involved. They've sent someone to check that he's safe and being treated well, but I think that's as far as they're prepared to go at this stage."

"So if we want my dad back we have to find a cool half million," I said.

"That's about the size of it," mum smiled weakly.

"So what do we do?" I asked. "We can't just sit here."

"We're doing what we can," Joan said in a more helpful manner. "I can't lay my hands on half a million, and as a matter of principle I'm not sure I would, even if I could. But your mother has asked if I'll help towards paying for a private detective she's found who can go out to Nicaragua and hopefully negotiate your father's release."

"I've spoken to him and he seems a very sensible, competent person with good contacts," mum said. "He used to be with some branch of the Metropolitan Police."

At which point Geraldine came in with a tray of tea things and a smirk on her face which clearly demonstrated that even if she hadn't heard all the details she knew that something was up and she was thoroughly enjoying herself. There was silence while she set tea, sandwiches, cakes and crockery on the table at the side of the room and then said to Joan "I'll see you tomorrow." She left without even looking at my mum and I, and even though there were far more important things on my mind I was reminded of how much I disliked her.

I helped Joan serve the tea and sandwiches and by the time we were all sitting down again the mood had somehow become a bit more normal and the conversation turned to more ordinary things, such as what I'd been up to. Uncle Frank arrived just in time to "refresh the pot", as he put it, and not for the first – or last – time I saw the amazing ability my family had to change the subject to something nicer and the mood to something lighter when they needed to.

But that's just a way of brushing stuff under the carpet, or bottling it up, and it all started to come out again once I'd gone to bed. I lay awake worrying about my dad until I was so tired I drifted off to sleep, but I drifted in and out of sleep all night. When I was sleeping I had horrible dreams which woke me up, and then I'd lie in my bed listening to the silence all around and my mind would go racing all over the place until I was too tired to think and I'd drift off to sleep again and be back in the nightmares.

9

I'd been instructed not to tell anyone about my dad, absolutely no one. Not any of my school friends, who I'd pretty much lost touch with by then anyway, not Miss Kimble, who I felt guilty about not keeping in touch with, not Sarah or Duncan or anyone else. So when I woke up properly at about five the next morning I lay staring up at the ceiling wondering how I was going to keep it from Sarah. I knew I wouldn't blurt something out and I probably wouldn't let anything slip, but she knew me well enough by then to know when something was wrong.

I could hear my mum snoring in the next room and outside the dawn chorus was getting louder so I wasn't likely to get back to sleep any time soon. I was wide awake, so I decided to go for a walk and clear my head.

The cold hit me as soon as I walked out through the back door. It was like a slap in the face with a bag of fresh air, but I was used to fresh air by then so it was quite invigorating. I decided to walk all the way around the lake, which would be a good few miles and would take a while, but I'd probably be back at about the time everyone else was down for breakfast. I walked very carefully past the bit where I fell over and a little while later found a path which, as it turned out, went almost all the way around the lake with just a few points where I had to go down onto the shore and risk getting my feet wet. All the way around the lake the water was to my left and the trees and hills to my right and there wasn't another human being in sight.

At least I couldn't see anyone else, but I had a feeling I was not entirely alone. I wasn't sure when I first noticed it but I became aware of a buzzing noise for some of the time. At first I thought someone might be cutting down trees with a chainsaw but who on earth would be cutting down trees at that time in the morning? And then I realised there'd be a buzz, a pause and then a crash as the tree came down but this seemed to be continuous. I couldn't hear it clearly all the time because the breeze, even though it was quite light, blew the sound away from me at some points and towards me at others. It seemed to be coming from the opposite side of the lake to where I was, and by the time I'd walked around to the other side it had stopped.

By then I could hear loads of birds singing in the trees, although I couldn't see many of them, but I did see what looked like an eagle high up above the lake at one point. It circled around a few times, dived down towards the shore on the far side but then veered off and flew away. Even at that distance it looked majestic and powerful, and as I watched it gliding with its wings spread wide I began to understand why so many people enjoy flying small planes. The world must look so different from up there, it must give you a different perspective on things. Perhaps all your problems disappear when you're that high up.

And that made me think about my dad, which I'd managed not to since I got dressed. I thought about him locked up in some filthy prison cell, unable to speak the language and hardly being fed. I was frightened for him, and the fear was worse because there was nothing I could do to help him.

I wondered what would happen if he never came back. I was used to him being away, but this was different. He was often away, sometimes for quite a while, but until now he'd always come back and when he did things were good and he was fun. I didn't know how my mum would cope if anything happened to him.

By then I was about two thirds of the way round the lake and the sun was getting higher. There was a clear, fresh amber light spreading through the trees and across the water which made everything look warmer than it probably was, and the water looked wonderfully blue. Usually it looked more grey than blue, especially by the afternoon when I normally went for a walk, but this was definitely a rich blue with maybe a hint of grey just beneath, and speckled golden amber light dancing on the surface. It gave me an idea for a painting, and I wondered if I could get that sense of the grey just underneath the blue but not impinging on it in any way.

That was when I noticed the waves. The lake was pretty much surrounded by trees and hills, which protected it for the most part from strong winds so the waves that came to the shore were quite gentle and sometimes barely noticeable. But there were waves in the middle of the lake, and they were more like the trail left in the water by a boat. It was as if something was travelling towards the island, but it was too small even to be a rowing boat. And there was no noise. The bird song had stopped and there was absolute silence. I couldn't see what was leaving the trail in the water because it must have been just under the surface, but it wasn't making a sound and then it just disappeared. Whatever made the waves must have been swimming just at the surface and now it had gone further down and within seconds there was no visible trace of where it had been.

It was too small for a boat, but too big to be a fish. And anyway, boats don't go below the surface, unless they're submarines, and fish don't swim that close to the surface. They swim beneath it, lower down. Whatever it was had been much closer to the surface than a fish would go. I stood for a while watching the water but didn't see anything else. Whatever it was had disappeared, just like the thing I saw on the edge of the island when I was on my way to Sarah's. At school we used to have a mad housemistress who swore blind that when she was a little girl in Ireland she was walking across a bridge early one morning when she realised a Leprechaun was sitting on the bridge watching her. She says as soon as she turned to look it disappeared because that's what Leprechauns do – they vanish as soon as they've been noticed. I began to feel a little uncomfortable about that. We made such fun of her whenever she told us that story. We thought we were doing it quietly behind her back but she probably knew and it suddenly seemed rather cruel. I was beginning to wonder if she'd been right after all.

When I got home Frank was making breakfast.

"Hello, sweetheart, have you been out?" he asked.

"That's why I'm just coming in," I replied.

"Oooh, that razor sharp wit! I wonder where you get it from! Get your coat off and you can come and help me."

Frank believed that the mere smell of his cooking was enough to get everyone up, and once again he was proved right. By the time I'd set the table and helped him a bit in the kitchen Joan and my mum were in the dining room and from what I could hear as I went in and out the conversation was not just about my dad but also about me and school and the future in general. And none of it sounded very positive.

When we were all sitting down I tried to change the subject by asking about the wildlife on the lake and the island. I told them about the eagle, which they said was unusual in that area, and they seemed really interested when I told them about the light and how I wanted to try to paint something that suggested the light dancing on the blue and grey of the water.

"Can you do that?" Joan asked me.

"How do you mean?"

"Have you got the materials, the space and the light and whatever else you need up in your room?"

"Oh, I thought you meant have I got the talent!"

"I'm assuming you have the talent, but do you have the wherewithal?"

"Well, yeah," I hesitated. "I think so, although those sketch books you got me are nearly full now and I'm getting through my paint supplies."

"And are we going to see what you've done so far?"

"I'll show you some of it after breakfast if you like," I said and she nodded. It was fair enough, I suppose, since she'd paid for them, but I didn't really like the idea of showing her what I'd done. I didn't think it was good enough and I felt a bit embarrassed.

"There was something else I saw on the lake that I wanted to ask you about," I said and I told them what I'd seen on the water as Frank got up to get more coffee.

"There are strange currents in the water," Joan said. "That's one reason I told you not to use the boat. Unless you know what you're doing those sudden currents can be very dangerous."

"I don't think it was a current," I said. "I think there was something just beneath the surface of the water and it was that, whatever it was, that was making the waves."

"Perhaps it was a fish," my mum suggested.

"It was just beneath the surface," I repeated and shook my head. "It can't have been a fish."

"A swimmer, then," Joan suggested and I almost laughed.

"In that water? At that time in the morning?"

"Believe me, there are plenty of lunatics who do such things," she said.

"There are hundreds of them every year in Windermere," Frank said as he came back with more coffee. "'Wild swimming', it's called. It's popular down at Loughrigg Tarn as well. Beats me why anyone would want to do it, but they do."

"Oh, there was another thing," I suddenly remembered. "There was a kind of buzzing I heard from time to time. Like a chainsaw only there wasn't a crashing sound so it wasn't trees being cut down."

"The only people allowed to cut the trees around here are the forestry commission," Joan said. "I suppose it's possible they were working early."

"You don't always hear the crash," Frank pointed out.

"Could it have been a boat, perhaps?" mum suggested. "Outboard motors make a buzzing noise, don't they?" I thought I saw Joan gave her a quick sharp look.

"The only boats on the lake are for pleasure," Frank said. "No one goes out on the water that early for pleasure. Too cold!" And with that he started to clear away the breakfast things, as if to bring the conversation to an end.

Frank seemed uncomfortable and that, in turn, made me uncomfortable. You know when an older person, a 'grown up', is telling you something and you have a sneaky feeling that whilst they're not exactly lying they're not telling you everything? If you do, you know how I felt and why I didn't feel I could push things any more just then.

The conversation turned to my dad. My mum felt she'd be better off going back home and 'directing operations', as she optimistically put it, from there. I offered to go with her but she said she'd have less to worry about if she knew I was safe up here. I could see her point, but I was worried about her being at home alone, worried and frightened, but she was certain I was better off with Joan and Frank. I wondered if it was more a case of her being better off without me. Just as well I don't take such things personally. She promised to keep more closely in touch from now on, though, which was something.

I sat in the back while Joan drove mum to Oxenholme. Hardly a word was said. It seemed that everything that could have been said had already been said, and anything else was perhaps best left unsaid. It was a slightly uncomfortable atmosphere, to say the least.

We got to the station just as the train was arriving so there wasn't much time for soppy goodbyes, which I'm not good at anyway. I gave her a hug and a kiss and again she promised to be in touch more than she had been. Then she told me I was the most precious thing in her world. I don't think she'd ever said anything quite like that to me before, I'd always assumed dad was more important to her, and so I didn't really know what to say. I just kissed her on the cheek and squeezed her arms. Then she picked up her case, kissed Joan on the cheek and got onto the train. She was still walking down the carriage looking for a seat as it pulled away so she didn't even wave goodbye. I felt another of those lumps in my throat – and a teeny weeny sense of impending doom in my heart.

Joan and I got back into the car, again without a word being spoken. It was only when we took a different turn and drove into Kendal that I asked where we were going.

"To sort you out,' she said rather cryptically. We pulled up in a supermarket car park and she marched straight past the supermarket entrance and turned into an alleyway of shops. I was about to ask what was happening when she said, "We'll go there for lunch when we've finished. We're not going to get into trouble, I've known the manager for years."

I bet you have, I thought.

I was struggling to keep up with her as she marched along the alleyway and then turned into a shop. A bell rattled as she pushed the door open and she said, "Here we are!" and for a moment I wondered if it was my birthday. It was an art supplies shop that was an Aladdin's cave full of stuff I would have loved to have. It had everything and anything an artist could ever possibly need, all crammed in so tightly it seemed as if the stock was spilling over onto the floor and climbing up the walls of its own volition.

An elderly man came out from the back and his face lit up when he saw Joan and rushed forward to greet her. "Hello, my darling!" he said as they gave each other a hug and a kiss on the cheek, "Where've you been?"

"Busy, my love," she replied.

"What? Too busy even to come and see your friends?"

"I'm here now and I need your help," she said. "This is my -" she paused for a second and then said the dread word "granddaughter," which made the old man laugh.

"I've heard a lot about you," he said as he shook my hand. "I'm Bill."

"Camille will be staying with me for a while and by all accounts Art is the only thing she's interested in at school, or indeed any good at from what I can gather." Thanks for that, dearest Grandmother, I thought, but Bill gave me a wink to say he knew what she was like. I took an instant liking to him. "So while she's with me she might as well continue with her art. So she needs…" she waved her hands vaguely around the shop and said "stuff". Then she turned to me and said, "Just help yourself to whatever you want, darling. Absolutely whatever."

"Anything?"

"Anything and everything," she emphasised. "Whatever you need, just help yourself." I looked around and didn't know where to begin.

"What do you like to work with, and on?" Bill asked.

"I draw a lot," I said and he pointed to one side of the shop. "But I also paint a lot." He pointed to the other side and I realised how well organised it all was.

"What do you paint with?" he asked.

"Acrylics. They don't let us use oils until we're in the sixth form," I realised I was speaking as if I was still at St. Dunstan's.

"Penny pinching," he tutted. "Most schools are like that. They don't let you use the expensive stuff until you're older and then you're suddenly expected to know how to use it straight away." I hadn't thought of it like that, but he was right. "Take some acrylics, by all means, but you need to get started on oils as soon as you can if you want to get the hang of it. It's completely different from working with acrylics, and you'll probably make a few mistakes at first, so take as much as you fancy." If I took all that I wanted it was going to be expensive but he could see what I was thinking and just said, "Oh, don't worry about the cost: your Grandmother's loaded and she gets the 'Old Flame' discount anyway." She laughed and then nodded at me to say it was all right.

Bill brewed a pot of tea and they sat and chatted while I piled stuff on to the counter and then on the floor and by the time I'd finished it all stretched half way to the door. She looked at it all and said, "You're sure that's everything?" I nodded. To be honest it was more than everything. There were canvasses and two different kind of easels and loads of sketchbooks and pads and watercolour paper and inks, pastels, pencils, watercolour paints, watercolour pencils and coloured pencils and loads of acrylics and oils and dozens of different brushes. It was more than I really had space for in my room, and it was probably more than a little greedy, but I didn't think I'd ever get a chance like that again and I knew I wouldn't be able to ask her for anything else in the future if I hadn't got it there and then. So I got it all there and then.

"Well then, tot it all up please, dearest," she told Bill, "and we'll be on our way." The final amount was huge but the discount was generous, which brought it down somewhat, and as Joan handed her credit card over to Bill she handed me the keys to the car. "You'll have to load it all," she said. "I'm too delicate and he can't leave the shop."

"I can close for a few minutes," he said. "Where are you parked?"

"Don't be silly," she said to him. "Some other fool might want to spend as much as I've just done and you'll miss them."

"They'll come back," he said, but she shook her head.

"She's fit and strong, she can do it herself," she said and that was the end of it.

I started to go back and forth between the shop and the car while they nattered away and paid no attention to me. It was odd hearing snippets of their conversation as I came in and out of the shop, and I got the impression they used to go out with each other, a long time ago, and had loads of friends in common. At one point when I came in he was telling her a story about meeting up with Frank at Carlisle races and whatever had happened had her in stitches, and by the time I got back from loading the next lot she was telling him about a day out she'd had with some friends in Blackpool. None of it made much sense to me, but then again I don't think it was meant to.

After I'd finished loading the car we said goodbye and Joan took me into the supermarket and downstairs to a really nice cafe and bought me an early lunch. "I have to go to the hotel after I've dropped you off," she explained, "and it might be late before I get back. Unless you're going over to Sarah's…"

"I'd rather get started with some of the stuff you've just bought me," I said and she smiled at what was obviously the right answer.

10

I must admit I was so excited with my new materials that I sort of avoided Sarah for a few days. I felt a bit bad about that but there was so much I wanted to do. In a way it didn't matter because it would soon be the end of term so we'd have plenty of time to spend together and I spoke to her on the phone a couple of times each day. I was really enjoying working with oils, and I was amazed at how different it was to using acrylics. It was almost like learning to paint again from scratch and I was loving it. I even changed my routine and went for walks in the early morning to see what the light was doing and then go home to try to catch it with paint.

I'd turned my room into a mini studio, with old sheets down over the carpets and the curtains taken down and put into the airing cupboard – partly to stop them getting covered in paint and partly to let as much light in to my room as possible. I was so excited I even let Joan come in now and again to see what I'd been doing. I'd been reluctant at first, not just because I wasn't sure it was any good but also because I thought she wouldn't like the way I was trying to create abstract paintings that got their inspiration from real places and things I'd actually seen, but she understood what I was trying to do and seemed genuinely to like it. Frank looked at some of it and said he liked it as well. "But it does leave me with one big question," he said as he looked at one of the canvasses with a rather worried expression.

"What's that?" I asked.

"Do we call you Pablo or Jackson?"

"We call me Camille," I said and they both smiled.

Again, the right answer.

And then it started to rain. And it rained and rained like nothing I've ever seen in my life before and I was stuck in the house for four days. The house Chris was working on had a flood because the wind blew some tiles off the roof so he was madly trying to sort that out and Joan and Frank had to help at the hotel because none of the guests could go out anywhere so they were staying in and eating and drinking loads because there wasn't much else for them to do. All of this was good for business, at least at the hotel, but it meant there was no one either Sarah or I could cadge a lift off so we couldn't see each other anyway.

All this helped take my mind off my dad to some extent, which was one of the reasons Joan had taken me to Bill's shop in the first place. Not seeing Sarah for a few days also meant that I'd be more used to the situation with my dad by the time I did see her, so hopefully she wouldn't notice anything odd and suspect I was upset or hiding something.

My mum phoned to tell us the detective, Mr Clements, was out there and had made contact with the embassy and the police. They still wanted half a million but he was hopeful they could be persuaded to drop the price. Hopefully to about a fiver, Frank said.

After a couple of days Sarah started to get a bit whiney and even though I knew she was laying it on thick I did feel a bit guilty when I got a voicemail in which she just said "Don't you want to be my friend any more? Don't you love me anymore?" in a really whiney wingeing voice so I phoned her back on the landline after supper.

"Where've you been?" she asked.

"Busy," I said. "I told you I had some art work to do."

"Oh yeah, for that school you're never going back to. I forgot. Listen. I've got three weeks to the end of term at that godforsaken hole of a school I still have to go to and then when I go back I only have another week and then I'm on study leave for the rest of the term, so we can have some fun!"

"Aren't you supposed to be revising?"

"Yeah, duh! But I'll have time for fun as well! What do you fancy doing?"

"I'll help you revise."

"God you're soooooo exciting! No wonder they chucked you out. We could go to Glastonbury!"

"Can't get tickets, don't have any money, and there's another reason. Let me think. Oh yeah! It's a three day mud pile full of old hippies and hedge fund managers pretending to be hippies."

"Oh, what is the matter with you, child? You're middle aged already and you're a year younger than me! Okay, if you don't want to go to Glasto here's a compromise: come and have dinner with my family tomorrow night. You can stay the night. We can have a sleepover! We can pitch the tent and have loud music and pretend we're at a festival!"

She didn't bother to mention that Duncan was home for a couple of days to report on something that was happening at Hawkshead. I felt myself blush as I walked into the house with my slightly girly luggage and the girly pyjamas that were in it, even though there was no reason why he would see them. I think it was because I remembered the thing about small furry animals when he took me home last time and felt a bit silly. And I knew the reason Sarah hadn't told me he was home was pure mischief. I suddenly didn't want to be sleeping in a tent in silly pyjamas if he was around, and it wasn't because I fancied him in any way, it was purely and simply because I didn't want him to think I was a silly girl. I didn't even raise the matter with Sarah because I knew she'd only take the mick and that would make things worse.

Denise had cooked chicken breasts wrapped in Parma ham and they were wonderful – almost as good as the way Perry did them at the hotel, but I told her they were just as good if not better and she looked pleased. Chris let us have a small glass or two of wine and when neither of them were looking Sarah topped us up once or twice, which I thought was silly because it would be obvious what she was doing when the bottle was suddenly empty, but she never seemed to think things through carefully.

While we were sitting in the dining room we could see the trees and plants in the garden being blown about by the wind and then the rain started, light at first but quickly getting heavier.

"Ha! There goes your sleepover!" Duncan said.

"No it doesn't," Sarah replied. "Cammy and I are made of sterner stuff than you think." I wasn't too keen on being called Cammy. It was girly and made me think of soap.

"It doesn't matter how tough you are I don't think you're going to be sleeping in that," Duncan pointed outside. We turned round to look and saw the tent had collapsed in a pool of muddy water with the rain falling even faster. Sarah groaned and Duncan laughed. "Looks like you didn't put the stakes in firmly enough or tie the guy ropes tight enough," he said.

"Oh, and you're such a camping expert?" Sarah said, but he just shook his head.

"I prefer to keep dry," he said. "My idea of the great outdoors is driving to a nice hotel with good rooms and a well stocked bar."

"In which case you can start by paying the bar bill here," Chris said as he held up the empty bottle. Duncan just shrugged and said, "I owe you," which I thought was pretty decent because by rights he ought to have blamed us.

It wasn't long after dinner that Chris and Denise said they needed an early night and left the three of us alone. Chris's parting words to Duncan were "Do not let these two have too much to drink. If Camille goes home tomorrow with a thick head mine will be on a plate." It was nice to be treated like a grown up but he needn't have worried. I got drunk at a christening party when I was in year 8 and didn't like it and felt awful the next day so ever since I've avoided that horrible feeling at all costs.

Sarah, on the other hand, was not so reserved. She insisted on opening another bottle "Go on, Duncan, he pretty much said we could…" and when that bottle was half finished so was she. By then we were sitting in the conservatory with the rain hammering down on the glass roof and Sarah fast asleep in one of the chairs. Duncan mentioned that he'd covered the opening of a school swimming pool the week before. "Not exactly the high point of my journalistic career," he said. "How much can you find to say about the opening of a swimming pool? The problem was I had to do a big feature on it because the school takes out a couple of full page ads each year for their open days so they're quite good customers."

"Oh, right!" I felt the urge to tease him. "So if you spend a lot of money with the papers you get better coverage, is that how it works?"

"It's the same all over the world, I'm afraid."

"Do you go swimming?" I asked.

"Used to, when I was a kid, not so much now. Why?"

"Did you ever swim in the lake?"

He laughed at the idea. "Leaving aside the fact that we were given strict instructions not to go anywhere near the island on pain of death, you must be kidding – it's freezing in there! I mean maybe in the middle of a really, really incredibly hot summer when the sun's shone on the water for hours at a time for days on end and there's not been a drop of rain and no drop in temperature, then yeah, I might possibly have gone swimming in it. But how often does that happen around here? Otherwise uh – uh," he shook his head.

"So would anyone be in the lake at about five in the morning at this time of year?"

"Only if they were completely insane, why?"

I told him what I'd seen the other morning and could have guessed his initial reaction. "So you think this is one of those small furry creatures you saw on the island last time I was home?" I felt embarrassed and he must have noticed. "No, I'm sorry," he said. "I know it sounds like I'm making fun of you but I'm not. Really, I'm not." He was quiet for a moment and then said, "Now that I think about it, when we were little we did play near the lake sometimes, even though we weren't supposed to, and a kid in our class told us he'd seen

116

something sliding into the water from the edge of the island and then disappear."

"Did he say what it was?" I asked.

"No," he shook his head. "To be honest he was always in trouble at school for telling lies so we thought he was just trying to frighten us and we ignored him," he smiled at the memory.

"Can you ask him now?" I asked, but again he shook his head.

"He moved away when we went up to secondary school. I've no idea where he is, and now I think of it I can't even remember his name."

"But what if he was telling the truth?" I asked. "What I saw in the lake was too big for a seal or an otter, but smaller than a rowing boat."

"Pine marten!"

"What?"

"It's a pine marten, most probably."

"What's a pine marten?"

"A slightly bigger furry animal!" he laughed. "It's about, I dunno, three feet long including the tail."

"That's smaller than a seal," I pointed out.

"But a bit bigger than an otter," he said. "They live in wooded areas so the island would be perfect but the big deal is they haven't been seen around here for years. They're mostly up in Scotland. If there's a family of them here that would be brilliant news for the Wildlife trust, and me!"

"Why you?"

"There's a story in it! Better than swimming pools."

"Oh, wow! Is this your big break into Fleet Street?"

"Of course not, but for round here it could be a big story. We need to find out."

"We?"

"Well you told me about it, so it's partly your story. It'll be good to feature you: 'The girl who found the pine martens'."

I wasn't sure I wanted the publicity, not with everything that was going on with my dad. It was more likely to complicate things.

"I dunno," I said, "it's your story now. I've given you the scoop."

"No, come on, it'll be fun. And anyway I need you to show me where you saw it."

"I probably imagined it."

"No you didn't. You saw something, and it's worth investigating. We can get up early and find it in the morning."

"Find what?" Sarah had woken up. Duncan explained. "How are we going to find it?" she asked.

"We'll get up early and try to photograph it."

"How early?" Sarah asked while Duncan looked at something on his phone.

"Here…" Duncan said, quoting from his phone. "They are mainly active at night and dusk…"

"How've you got a signal?" Sarah asked.

"I keep telling you, you get what you pay for in life. Now listen. 'They have small, rounded, highly sensitive ears and sharp teeth adapted for eating small mammals, birds, insects, frogs, and carrion. Yeah, yeah, blah, blah' he was flicking through the entry looking for relevant bits. 'European pine martens are territorial animals that mark their range by depositing faeces called 'scats' in prominent locations'."

"I know a chambermaid who does that with radios," I said.

"Huh?" they both asked.

"Never mind, carry on," I said.

"'These scats are black and twisted and can be confused with those of the fox, except that they reputedly have a floral odour.' Ah, that's nice. A-ha! Listen to this: 'Although they are preyed upon occasionally by golden eagles, red foxes, wolves and wildcats, humans are the largest threat to pine martens.' So they could well be flourishing on the island," he said.

"I also saw an eagle at the same time," I said. "I hope the eagle didn't catch it."

"We've all got to eat," Duncan said, not very helpfully. "Now if they're mainly active at night and dusk perhaps we should be out there now."

"What, in the dark?" Sarah moaned. "On your own, mate."

"But if Camille saw one early in the morning that would be a better time to photograph it. We should go to bed now and get up at four and go straight there to have a look."

"Without any breakfast?" Sarah sounded horrified.

"We can get some when we get back. In fact, I'll tell you what: if we find what we're looking for I'll take the pair of you to Howgate for breakfast." I looked at Sarah for an explanation.

"It's a hotel that does probably the best breakfasts in Cumbria, but even so..."

"It'll be worth it," Duncan promised us.

"But how are we going to get to the island?" Sarah asked. "We don't have a boat."

"Tod Simpson does," Duncan was getting really fired up with enthusiasm. "It's moored on a little jetty on the far side from Joan and Frank's."

"The green one?" I asked and he nodded. "I've seen it."

"He covers it with a tarpaulin and leaves it tied to the jetty. It's easy to start and I know what to do."

"He'll kill you," Sarah pointed out in a deadpan voice.

"He won't know. It'll be back in place before he comes anywhere near it and we'll have used hardly any fuel."

"I don't like this, Duncan," Sarah said.

"Neither do I," I added but he just looked at me with mock horror.

"You started this – you have to go with me!" Then he told Sarah, "You can wait on the shore if you're worried. Keep watch."

Sarah nodded and said, "You're big brother. On your head be it."

11

I'm sure I'd only just closed my eyes when the alarm on my phone went off. Sarah had put out some clothes for me to borrow before we went to bed and we got dressed and went downstairs very quietly without a word being spoken. Duncan made some coffee, which we drank in silence and then we crept out of the house and closed the door quietly behind us. The rain had finally stopped but the path to the car, the car itself and the roads were all wet and slippery and in the grey early morning light I didn't really want to go. I would rather have just gone back to bed, and it might have saved a lot of trouble all round if we had.

No one said a word as Duncan started up the engine and drove off carefully. I don't know about the others but I had a strange sense of foreboding. Maybe it was because we were so tired or because in the light of day this seemed to be not such a good idea. Now I think back, it was probably both.

We drove for just a few minutes and then reached a lay-by. From there it was a short walk through some trees and down a slightly uneven path to the lake. By then the light was clear and the water was so calm that the lake looked quite majestic and I felt rather proud that I lived right by it. But it was cold, as I knew it would be.

About two hundred yards over to our right was a little jetty, carefully painted in white, and closely tied to it was Tod Simpson's little green boat. What I didn't realise at the time was that the jetty was at the bottom of Tod's garden and, technically, simply being there meant we were trespassing. The tarpaulin covering the boat was dangling into the water at the edges so as we lifted it up and away from the boat water drained down onto our legs and feet and it was so icy cold to the flesh it was like an electric shock. We dragged the tarpaulin over to the edge of the jetty and went back to the boat. Duncan said almost the first word of the morning.

"Damn."

"What?" Sarah asked.

"The outboard's not there. There's just a couple of oars."

"Can you row?" I asked.

"Anyone can row," he sounded cocky but I could tell he was worried.

"Well I can't," I thought I'd better make that clear from the outset.

"Don't worry, I'll do it," he said. Then he turned to his sister and asked, "You sure you don't want to come with us?" She shook her head silently. "Okay, just keep watch. Shout if there's a problem. We'll be as quick as we can."

Duncan knelt on the jetty and held the boat as I climbed in. It rocked from side to side with every slight movement and I was uncomfortably aware that this rather unstable little pile of wood was all there was between me and that icy cold water. I sat on a little ledge at the back while Duncan climbed in and stood rather unsteadily as he untied the rope from the jetty and pushed the boat away into the water. Even the process of him sitting down and picking up the oars made the boat rock unpleasantly, but once he got into his stride things seemed to settle down. He picked up a steady rhythm with the oars and the water seemed calm again.

I had no idea how long it would take to reach the island, and to this day I have no idea how long it actually took. It seemed to take for ever. For a while it seemed as if we were getting nowhere. Despite all the effort Duncan was putting into it we hardly seemed to be moving at all. I wondered if his claim that anyone could row was just bravado and that he actually had no idea what he was doing.

But then the island looked as if it was moving closer to us, rather than us moving towards it. I nodded towards it and Duncan looked over his shoulder and when he saw how close we were he turned back to me a gave me a beaming smile.

"Not so bad, was it?" he asked quietly.

"No, but we've got to get back yet," I pointed out.

We got out and dragged the boat the last few yards onto the island. I could feel the water through my boots and the bottoms of my jeans and my feet squelched as we walked.

I don't know what I was expecting, but the island was a bit of a disappointment. It was wildly overgrown in a way that was disturbing rather than romantic. The sign warning us of the dire consequences of being there looked old and shabby. The wood was beginning to rot at the edges and the paint was peeling and fading. No one had done anything to it for years and as we walked further on it looked as if no one else had been on the island for ages. The ground was thick with bracken and ferns and dangerously uneven. After we'd walked through the undergrowth for a few minutes I realised one of the things that was unsettling about the place was there were no paths. I'd never been for a walk in the woods without even a path before, even the walks I took over the hills every day followed paths. This was different. Here, I realised, you really could get seriously lost.

Further in there were huge, thick thorny brambles which rose up to a height of about ten feet and we had to fight our way through by pulling our sleeves over our hands. By then we knew we'd come ridiculously unprepared. My feet were still cold and squelching and my hands and arms were scratched and bleeding. I was about to say something like we ought to have brought gloves and knives but there was no point in saying it. It was obvious.

And water. It was still early and not very warm, but I was already getting thirsty.

And then there were the trees. There must have been hundreds, if not thousands, of them. I'm not good at spotting trees but I knew most of these were pines of one kind or another, tall and dark with scaly barks and needles rather than leaves. They were close together and other greenery had wrapped itself around first one tree and then along a branch and on to another, making walking between trees quite difficult. The island was like this because no one had done anything with it and now it was in a state where no one could do anything with it. It was just a very unwelcoming overgrown mess.

"This is not a good place for a picnic," Duncan said cheerfully as he climbed through some more bracken ahead of me. "I won't be coming back in a hurry."

"I don't even know what we're looking for," I said.

"They make dens in hollowed trees or undergrowth. I haven't seen any hollowed trees and this undergrowth is so thick I doubt we'd ever find anything."

It seemed now as if the island was bigger than it appeared to be from a distance. We trudged on for about half hour before I asked, "Do you think we're lost?"

"Not exactly lost," he paused while I caught up with him. "But I've no real sense of where we are. Have you?" I shook my head and thought that a compass would have been useful. I was getting tired and fed up. "In theory if we keep walking we'll come to one side of the island or the other eventually and be able to make our way back to the boat just by walking around the edge," he said.

"Can we do that, please?" I asked. "I'm thirsty and getting tired." I was also beginning to feel weak with hunger.

"Come on, then," he said and pointed to his right, "I reckon we need to go that way." He was trying to look confident but I was sure it was just to make me feel more optimistic. I don't think he felt any better than I did.

We'd got about ten yards further when I heard a kind of snorting noise and something rushed past me through the undergrowth. I caught just a glimpse of something for a split second and I yelped in surprise as it disappeared.

"What is it?" Duncan asked.

"There's a pig!" I shouted.

He stopped and turned back to me. "Really?" He asked.

"It went that way," I pointed over to my left.

"Let's see if we can find it. If there isn't a story in this at least there's a competition: 'Name That Pig'."

We set off in pursuit, listening carefully as we went. A couple of minutes later we both heard the snuffling sound.

"That's not like any pig I've ever heard," Duncan almost whispered. "It sounds more like a walrus." Ahead of us the undergrowth shivered as whatever it was ran further towards the centre of the island. "Come on," he said, "let's follow it!"

The chase, for want of a better word, gave me a new wave of energy and although I was still aware of the squelching and discomfort it was a little easier to ignore. What we couldn't ignore, though, were the fallen trees we had to leap or climb over and the knots of overgrowth we had to kick through and each time we did we had to take our eyes off the movement ahead and within a few minutes we were deeper in the island with no sign of whatever we'd been chasing.

"I think we've lost it," I said as my eyes scanned the ground ahead of me.

"I think it went through the gap between those trees," he pointed. "Let's have a look and if we can't find it we give up and go back." He set off, and I followed reluctantly. I was tired again, and beginning to feel foolish, while he was already some way ahead.

"Oh my God, look at this!" he called as he came to a halt between the trees. I caught up and stood alongside him. It was a clearing. Quite a large one, where dozens of trees had been cut down and cleared away and, by the looks of it, the wood had been used to create a kind of cabin on stilts about six or seven feet above ground level with a wide stepladder leading up to a platform that went all around it.

"What is this?" I asked.

"Looks like the ultimate tree house," Duncan said quietly.

"Do you think anybody's here?" I whispered.

"Doesn't seem to be," he said. We listened carefully and heard nothing. "Come on, let's have a look," he said and went over to the steps.

"Are you sure it's safe?" I called.

"Nope," he said as he warily placed one foot and then another on alternative rungs. When he was half way up he called across to me, "It should be okay, the wood's not in bad nick and you're lighter than me. And anyway, if it all falls apart it's not that much of a drop to the ground."

"Far enough to break your neck," I pointed out.

By then he was at the door to the cabin. "Seriously, you're going to want to see this," he called over his shoulder.

The steps looked rickety and slightly rotten from a distance, but he was right: closer up they weren't so bad. At least I hoped not. I mounted them carefully and stood beside him at the doorway looking in to the cabin. There was a damp and rather musty smell. The roof was made from planks of wood and in one corner some of them had split and the rain had dripped in and was starting to rot the floorboards. On one side there was a small kitchen area and on the other a camp bed up against the wall. The floor was mostly bare wood, but in the middle of the room it was covered by an old rug which had seen better days. On the rug were a couple of old armchairs with a coffee table between them. The whole place looked as if it had been abandoned years ago.

Except for the bottle of single malt whisky on the table, which I knew from the label was quite new.

"What is this place?" I whispered.

"A story," he said as he started photographing it from all angles with his phone.

"How do you know?"

"I can feel it in my bones."

"I don't like it here," I said, fully aware of how pathetic that sounded.

"Somebody lived or stayed here, probably a long time ago. So what were they doing on an island that was supposed to be uninhabited and dangerous?" he asked aloud.

"I think we should go," I said.

"Why? There's nobody here but us."

"What makes you think that?" I asked. I was beginning to wonder if the pursuit of a story was getting in the way of his common sense.

"If anyone was here we'd have seen or heard them by now," he said.

"Don't be stupid!" I couldn't believe what he was saying. "We've never been here before in our lives and we don't even know exactly where we are on the island. We might not even be able to find our way back to the boat," I paused to let that sink in and then continued. "But someone – we've no idea who

– but someone," I emphasised, "has left a bottle of whisky here. Which means they'll be back. How do we know they're not watching us right now?"

That was one of those times when you only really know what you've said when you hear yourself saying it out loud, and when I heard myself saying it I realised how dangerous this could be and how frightened I ought to be. But it did the trick.

"Come on, then," he said and turned to go. Being not much of a gentleman he went first and I followed but then he stopped at the top of the stairs and I almost slammed into the back of him.

"For goodness' sake!" I said but he held up an arm to shush me and pointed towards the edge of the clearing. When I saw what he was pointing at my blood ran cold. We probably wouldn't have noticed if we'd been on the ground but from above we could see two darker patches where the earth had been dug over.

"Are they what I think they are?" I asked quietly.

He nodded. "I think so," he almost whispered.

"We need to go," I said, and this time he didn't argue.

We ran down the stairs and back the way we'd come, jumping over fallen trees and hacking at the overgrowth as it seemed to lurch towards us. It almost seemed as if, having seen what we'd seen, the island itself didn't want us to go, didn't want us to tell anyone else. By now the sun was quite high and the day was getting warm. I could feel the sweat forming on my back and trickling down my spine as we ran and although it was horribly uncomfortable I didn't care. I didn't care about anything as long as I got off that island.

About ten minutes later we came out of the undergrowth and found ourselves on the side looking towards Joan's house. We'd gone completely wrong somewhere and now had to walk back around the island. Slowing down a little to get our breath we still walked briskly back to where we'd left the boat and all I could do was hope and pray that we hadn't been seen from the house. When we reached the boat we found a new wave of energy which helped us lift it up and into the water and then jump in ourselves as it started to float away.

We could see Sarah at the edge of the lake and she waved to us once we were away from the island. I waved back while Duncan rowed but then she waved again, and I thought she just having a laugh.

"I'll buy you breakfast, like I promised," Duncan said. "We've got a lot to talk about, and you were brave to come with me." A tad patronising, I thought, but I let it pass. "Braver than my sister, certainly," he said as he looked around to see her waving again. "Now what's she doing?" he asked.

"I thought she was just being silly but I think she's trying to attract our attention." She was.

As I looked again I realised she wasn't simply waving, she was pointing at something over to my right, but I couldn't see what. I scanned the edge of the lake but all I could see were the few houses dotted around, one of which was Joan's, and again I hoped she didn't just happen to be looking out of a window at that moment.

I looked back to Sarah and she was even more frantic.

And then I saw it.

A line in the water, like I'd seen the other morning. The trail of something swimming just beneath the surface. As I traced the line to the point where it began I realised it was coming straight towards us and before I could warn Duncan it hit the boat with a huge and powerful slam. I saw the shock on Duncan's face as the boat tipped over and we were thrown into the lake.

They say your whole life passes in front of you as you drown and I know why. In the first few seconds the shock of being under freezing cold water made it seem almost as if I was outside myself and watching everything from a distance. My heart was beating frantically. I couldn't see a thing and I knew I couldn't survive in the water for very long. I still don't understand how water can be that cold without being ice.

I'd swallowed some water as I went under and my instinct was to cough but I knew I had to hold my breath and float back up to the surface first without coughing and without banging my head on the boat. I raised my arms above me for protection.

When I reached the surface I coughed and spluttered horribly but got my breath back and looked around me. The boat was further away than I'd expected and there was no sign of Duncan. I tried to swim to the boat but my clothes were heavy and weighing me down. I didn't know whether it was me not moving with the weight of my clothes or that the boat was moving further away from me but either way I didn't seem to be getting anywhere and I could feel a sense of panic building up inside me. I trod water for a moment and tried to think things through instead of worrying about reaching the boat. I took deep, steady breaths which helped quell the fear that I knew was the cause of the rising panic. I needed to be able to think straight, and that meant letting go of the fear.

I watched the boat bobbing gently on the water and realised the waves had subsided and the water was calm again. By some miracle the boat was upright. I knew I needed to get out of the water and into the boat because I could feel the cold not just on my skin but sinking into my whole body and the longer I stayed in the water the more likely I was to die. I had to get to that boat. Even if I couldn't climb back into it if I could hang on to it until help arrived I might be okay.

Then I realised help must be on its way because Sarah would have seen what happened. I just had to wait, but I couldn't wait long. I had to get to the boat, and I couldn't do that with my jacket, it was restricting my arms too much. I unfastened the jacket and let it float away and then I took off the sweater Sarah had lent me and let that float away as well. I remember thinking that was a shame because it was a nice sweater and Sarah would be cross and then I laughed at myself for worrying about something so trivial when I was about to die. I wanted to dump my jeans as well so I could move my legs more freely but that would involve taking off my boots and I didn't think I could do that, so I had to rely mostly on the strength in my arms to get me to the boat.

I started swimming again and it was a bit easier. Still difficult, and slow, but easier. A moment later Duncan surfaced almost beside me.

"You all right?" he asked as he spat water out over his shoulder. All I could do was nod. "Keep going," he said, "you're doing brilliantly." Again, I know he meant to be encouraging but it seemed patronising and if I didn't have bigger things on my mind just then I'd have given him what for. We swam beside each other for another minute or so and by then we'd almost reached the boat. "I'll go round the other side," he said. "If we try to get in on just on one side it'll tip the boat over." He dived below the boat and then I heard him coming up on the other side. "Ready?" he called.

"Think so," I replied rather weakly. I really wasn't sure if I could do this and it came across in my voice, I know.

"Try not to worry," he said. "We'll be out soon. After three. One – Two – Three!" He pulled himself up on his side of the boat but I wasn't ready, wasn't quick enough, and the boat tipped towards him and knocked him back into the water. I heard him swear. I didn't blame him.

"I'm sorry, that was my fault," I said. "Shall we try again?"

"Okay, ready?"

"Yes," and this time I was. I didn't want to let him down again, and I needed to be out of the water.

"On three, then. One – Two – THREE!"

It was the most physically demanding thing I have ever done in my entire life.

Like running a marathon and leaping the triple jump all within a single moment of supreme effort as, with more strength than I realised I had, I pulled as hard as I could to lift my soaking wet and heavy body up and away from the water. For a second Duncan mirrored me on the other side as we pushed down hard on the edge of the boat to raise ourselves to the point where we could fall into it. I rolled my legs in after me and then lay panting for breath. I was unbelievably cold and horribly wet but at least we were out of the water. We were alive.

Unless my grandmother killed me, of course.

I heard the outboard motor buzzing as her boat came towards us. I barely had the strength to lift myself up to see but I knew I had to and there, thank God, was Frank in the boat with Sarah. At least it wasn't Joan, I thought, but that just meant the worst was yet to come.

I realised then how long we'd been in the water. Long enough for Sarah to run like hell around the edge of the lake to Joan's house, hammer on the door until Frank appeared, help him open up the boathouse and get the boat started and out onto the water. That was a long time and I knew then I was very lucky to still be alive. By then I could see that Frank was in his dressing gown. He hadn't even bothered to get dressed. I was lucky to be alive and I was lucky to have someone who cared for me that much and reacted that quickly.

Frank and Sarah came alongside us and Sarah threw a rope to her brother, who fastened it at the front of Tod's boat. Once it was secure they sped off, Frank operating the outboard motor, and with a yank the rope tightened and our boat followed theirs to the other side of the lake.

Joan was waiting at the shoreline. She stood perfectly still and impassive and looked scarier than ever as we approached. As we reached the shore Duncan started to unfasten the rope but Frank told him not to bother. "I've got to take this back to where it belongs," he said, "and then I've got to find Tod."

We got out of the boat and waded through the water while Frank helped Sarah out of Joan's boat. When the three of us stood in front of her she finally acknowledged our presence.

"You need to get out of those clothes as quickly as you can," she said. "Come with me." With that she turned and walked briskly up towards the house. We followed her, water dripping off us and squelching in our boots and clothes. We didn't even speak to each other. I felt like the naughtiest child who'd ever been born and I'm sure they felt the same. This time I really was in trouble. When we reached the house she said to me, "Take Duncan up to the bathroom and sort him out some towels and a robe." She told Duncan, "Have a long bath, you need to warm through." Then she turned to me and said, "You can use my bathroom."

"I've got my own shower," I reminded her.

"You need a long soak in a hot bath," she said. "Hypothermia kills."

12

I took as long as I could in the bath. Partly because I realised how good it was for me to warm up throughout and partly because – obviously – I didn't want to go downstairs.

Ever.

By the time I was dressed and plucked up the courage to go down Chris had picked up the other two and Frank was over at Tod's. The house seemed empty and deathly quiet as I walked into the living room. Joan was sitting on one of the sofas and pointed me towards the other. I sat down and she looked straight at me for what seemed like forever. I knew there was no point in trying to start the conversation, what could I say? I'd been in situations like this often enough at school to know it's best just to sit tight and wait for whatever's coming to come, for come it will. Even so, this was worse than anything I'd ever had at school. When it came to creating an atmosphere every nun I'd ever met was a total amateur compared to my Grandmother.

Eventually she spoke.

"When I told you not to use my boat I assumed a girl of your intelligence would understand I meant I didn't want you to use anybody's boat".

"I know," I said. "I'm really, very sorry."

"That's not going to be enough," she said. "I specifically told you not to go on the lake and you disobeyed my instructions." Again there was no point in saying anything. She was completely in the right and I felt not just caught out, not just in trouble, but completely crushed, as if a wave of depression, sadness and guilt was weighing down on me. Then she said, "Not only have you disobeyed my instructions you have committed an act of trespass and an act of theft."

"We were only intending to borrow it," I said. "Tod wouldn't even know."

"He knows now, and he has every right to report you to the police."

"I'll go and apologise to him myself," I said.

"You will," she nodded. She wasn't acknowledging what I'd said so much as instructing me. "Which leads to my next question: why did you steal Tod's boat?"

I explained as best I could about what I'd seen on the water, what Duncan thought it might be and how there might be a story in it for him. Her eyes narrowed and her expression hardened as she listened.

"So you've been on the island?" she asked. I nodded. "Did I not specifically tell you that you must not, ever, under any circumstances, go onto that island?"

"I'm sorry," I said, nodding again. She didn't even acknowledge the apology.

"Why did you disobey me?" I took a deep breath and wanted to answer but realised there was nothing I could do or say that would make things any better. I gave up, and the breath came out as a long sigh. "Where did you go?" she asked.

"We landed on the opposite side to here," I said. "Obviously we didn't want you to see us," I shrugged.

"Obviously," she said. It felt as if the room was getting colder every time she spoke.

"And then we went towards what we thought was the middle -"

"Did you not have a compass with you?" I shook my head, and remembered what she'd said about idiots setting off without the right gear. "So you've no idea where you were." Again a statement, not a question. I nodded mutely. "What did you see?"

I told her about the pig, and how Duncan thought there might be a story in that and so we followed it to the clearing. When I mentioned the clearing there was a slight raising of one of her eyebrows, but all she said was, "Go on."

I told her about the cabin and I knew from the look on her face she knew about it already.

"What else?" she asked, and I knew what she meant.

"When we were on the platform outside we could see patches of disturbed earth," I said. "We thought they looked like shallow graves."

"Very observant of you," she said. "That's exactly what they are."

My heart leaped. She didn't move, show any expression, she didn't even bat an eyelid but my heart was racing and I suddenly saw her in a different light and began to understand. This was why my dad never got on with her, and why people called her 'The Godmother'. All the local connections she has; all the people who seem to do whatever she wants them to; the people who make a joke of being frightened of her; the people who owe her money; the people who seemed to live in her pocket.

This would explain everything.

I was so shocked and horrified my jaw must have dropped because the next thing she said was, "Close your mouth, child, you look gormless." I closed it and she stood up. "Give me your phone and laptop," she ordered.

"The phone's useless, it got wet when I was in the water."

"Nevertheless, give them to me." She followed me up to my bedroom and stood in the doorway holding out her hand. I handed over the phone and the laptop and she said, "You must not communicate with anybody, not even your mother, until I've decided what to do with you."

'With you', I noted.

Not 'about' you.

'With' you.

As in shallow graves, I couldn't help thinking.

"I hate to do this almost as much as I shouldn't have to do this," she continued, "but I must now insist that you stay in your room until further notice. You can do whatever you wish in here, as long as it does not involve contacting anybody else, but you do not leave this room until I say you can."

"What about food?"

"I will bring your lunch on a tray, and when I've gone back to the hotel Geraldine will bring you your supper." Oh, brilliant, I thought. Just what I need. "And in case I haven't yet made myself quite clear," she continued, "any further disobedience on your part will result in you literally having hell to pay. Is that quite clear?" I nodded. "Good," she said. She closed the door behind her and went back downstairs.

I think it was the way she closed the door. It seemed somehow so final. There were no locks or bars or barriers but I immediately felt as if I was under house arrest. I had nothing to complain about, and no one to blame but myself, but the sense of not being able to leave your own room, especially when it's not actually, really, really, your room in the first place, starts to get to you quite quickly. I lay on the bed, staring up at the ceiling, and thought how much worse it must be for my dad, wherever he was.

For lunch she brought up a bowl of Frank's soup with a couple of rolls and some fruit. Again, I couldn't complain. It was better than I'd get in a real prison, and much better than dad was probably getting, but not being able to leave my room and not knowing how long this would go on for left me feeling utterly helpless.

When she came to collect the tray I thanked her and said how good the soup was. "He's well known for it," she told me. "He makes vast quantities at a time, keeps it in the freezer and takes it round when any of our friends are ill." She paused and then added, "There are some who say it's so nourishing it can bring the dead back to life." I really didn't know how to take that. Was it a veiled threat of some kind, a reference to the graves on the island, or was she just playing with me?

Not long after that she went out – didn't bother to say goodbye – and I was left in the care of the lovely Geraldine, who later on brought up a casserole sent over by Perry for my supper. It was delicious, the whole thing only slightly soured by the smug look on her face as she handed the tray to me. I don't know how much she knew, but she knew enough to be really enjoying herself.

Once she'd left – again without saying goodnight or anything – I had a long, boring evening on my own. At about ten the home phone rang. I was tempted to answer it just in the hope of having a civilized conversation with someone but the chances were that whoever was calling wanted to speak to Joan or Frank and would at some point mention that I'd answered and I'd get into even more trouble, so I let it ring. And it rang and rang and rang and rang so I assumed it was important. It could have been Joan trying to contact me after all. It stopped ringing and then started to ring again almost immediately. I guessed it was the same person and it was important they spoke to someone. It might have been my mother with news of my dad. Hell, it might even have been my dad, so at that point I decided it was probably better, under the circumstances, to answer it after all.

It was Sarah.

"Thanks to you and my stupid brother I am deep in the mire!" She was not, as they say, a happy bunny, but I doubted she had as much to complain about as me.

"I'm sorry," I said, already worried about what might happen if Joan suddenly came home.

"But why me?" she asked. "What did I do? All I did was sit on Tod's little jetty and run like hell to get help to save your rotten lives, and for that I'm grounded for two weeks. My dad's taking me to and from school until the end of term then I have a whole week at home just working. Thanks a lot, mate!"

"I'm sorry, but it wasn't my idea."

"So? You're supposed to be intelligent. My brother's an idiot and you should have been able to talk him out of it."

"How is he?"

"Behaving very weirdly. I don't know what you two got up to on that island but I've never seen him so happy. What did you get up to?"

"Nothing," I said.

"You don't have to marry him just 'cos you had

a snog on a deserted but not at all tropical island, you know."

"We didn't!"

"Or worse."

"Stop it! We didn't do anything!"

"Then what's he so excited about?"

"I don't know," I said. "He thinks there might be a pig on the island and there's a story in it."

There was a pause, and then she said, "Really?"

"Yes, really."

Another pause and then, "My God, it's worse than I thought. He really is pathetic."

"Can I talk to him?" I asked.

"No."

"Now who's being pathetic?"

"You can't talk to him because he's not here, you idiot. He's gone back to work. Full of the joys of journalism."

I didn't want him to write anything. Anything he wrote would only get me into more trouble with Joan. I needed to talk to him, find out what he was intending to write and put him off for a while. "He owes us breakfast," I said. "When's he coming back?"

"You'll have to talk to him about that," she replied. "And you'll have to talk to me for the next two weeks because I can't see you. What did the Godmother say?"

Under the circumstances I opted for understatement. "She is seriously not at all impressed with me."

"You grounded?"

"I'm not supposed to leave my room and she's taken my phone and laptop."

"Good God, she's worse than my dad!"

A pair of headlights swung across the hall and I recognised the sound of Frank's car. "I have to go," I said. "Please explain to Duncan that I can't phone him and ask him to phone me in a day or two."

"Woo! You got it bad, girl!"

I had to let that one pass, put the phone down and run back up to my room.

I got onto my bed just as the front door opened and I heard Frank coming up the stairs and go into his room. He came out a few minutes later and knocked on my door. When I said, "Come in" he popped his head round.

"You all right?" he asked.

"Yep," I nodded. "I'm just really sorry." It was his turn to nod, and I could see he knew I meant it.

"I've persuaded Tod to put it all down to youthful high jinks and told him you'll be round yourself soon to apologise." I nodded and then he added, "He says if you're going to start messing about with boats you need to know what you're doing and he's offered to teach you how to row and how to use the outboard. I'd take him up on that if I were you,"

"If she ever lets me out of here I will," I nodded. "Is she still angry?"

He nodded again. "This is serious," he said.

"So what's going to happen?"

"I think she's going to talk to you in the morning. I suggest you try to get some sleep. Night night." Then he was gone and, once again, I was alone in that room. Very, very alone.

13

The light from the landing woke me up as Joan opened my bedroom door and stood in the doorway. I felt groggy and a little apprehensive. "What time is it?" I asked.

"Early," she said. "I want you to dress warmly and come downstairs." By then I was awake enough to smell coffee. Yes, I know, I really did wake up and smell the coffee.

It was as silent as a graveyard downstairs but I sensed a softening in Joan's attitude, albeit a very slight one. She was standing in the kitchen with a cup of coffee and pointed to another on the table. "Drink it quickly and get your boots and jacket on," she said. "We need to be off soon."

"Where are we going?" I asked.

"To the island," she said in a tone that suggested it was a stupid question. I frowned, and probably looked a bit stupid, and she said, "Frank and I have talked about this, and we think it's time you were properly admitted to the family business."

I didn't like the way she said that. What did being 'properly admitted' involve? And what exactly was 'The Family Business'? Bumping people off and burying them in shallow graves? I felt uncomfortable but I knew I had no choice.

As soon as I'd got my boots and jacket on she led me across the garden to the boathouse. "Hang on to this," she said as she handed me her rucksack and disappeared inside. A moment later the doors opened and she slid the boat down to the lake. "Get a move on," she gestured towards the boat. "We haven't got all day."

I sat at the front – the bow – and she sat at the stern. She started up the outboard motor and we sped off across the lake surprisingly quickly, the boat bouncing up and down on waves I couldn't even see. She didn't speak, and I just looked around me. Dawn had broken and apart from us there seemed to be nothing else around. I couldn't hear anything for the sound of the engine which, I realised, was the buzzing I'd heard when I'd gone for an early walk the morning after my mum turned up. The time I saw the wake of something swimming just under the surface of the water. It had to be more than a coincidence, it had to have been the same boat, but I couldn't imagine why my Grandmother had been on a boat on the lake so early in the morning – at least I couldn't imagine any nice, sane, rational, and innocent reason. I wondered how many other unexpected skills and talents she was going to turn out to have.

On the far side of the island from the house there was an inlet which created a natural point to come ashore without being seen. There was even a makeshift kind of jetty to secure the boat. There still didn't seem to be a path as such but she led me along a much easier route towards the middle of the island. It all seemed so simple and straightforward if you knew what you were doing that I felt embarrassed about the ham-fisted way Duncan and I had done things.

"Here we are," she said almost cheerfully as she held back some brambles and I was surprised to find we were in the clearing. She led the way past the graves, up the steps and into the cabin.

"What is this place?" I asked as we walked inside.

"All in good time," she said. "Sit."

I sat.

So did she.

I looked around the cabin, as much to avoid her gaze as anything else, but became uncomfortably aware that she was just watching me. Eventually I turned to look at her and the two of us sat for a minute (another long one) eyeballing each other. If it was anyone else, anywhere else, I'd have said it was childish and probably laughed, but with her it was freaky. It seemed as if she was trying to work something out, or measuring me out. I felt like a mouse cornered by a cat, unable to do anything. Unable to get away, entirely at the cat's mercy.

"This place was built years ago," she said eventually. As soon as she broke the silence I felt an amazing sense of relief and realised I'd been holding my breath.

"By you and Frank?" I asked, but she shook her head.

"Not exactly," she said. "Friends of ours, let's say." That sounded a bit dodgy. "It's beginning to fall apart now, but that doesn't matter. By the time it does we won't be needing it anymore." That, too, sounded slightly menacing. There were a lot of questions I could and should have asked, and it seemed as if she wanted me to ask them, but quite honestly I wasn't sure I wanted to hear the answers. "And it's a long time since anyone's slept here," she added. "I doubt anyone ever will again. I shouldn't think so, anyway."

I had to ask, "Who did sleep here?"

"An old friend of ours. A man called Eurof." She saw the look on my face and explained, "He was Welsh." I'd never heard the name before – sorry if you're Welsh, by the way. Oh, and if you've not heard it before it's pronounced 'Eye – Roff'

"Is he buried outside?" I asked.

"No, of course not. He's in the church yard. You have to register the deaths of people and give them a proper decent burial of some kind, you know." Well, yes, I knew that, but I've also seen movies where people are buried in the foundations of roads and buildings or dumped in lakes and rivers, so under the circumstances I thought it was a reasonable question.

"So who is buried outside?" I asked again.

She almost laughed as she said, "No one." Obviously that didn't make sense because she'd already said they were graves. She sat looking at me, waiting for me to speak. I'd realised some time ago that a lot of people respected her rather than loved her, and I could see why this was the case. She was playing a game with me, stretching something out to the point where it was unbearable, seeing if I'd crack first and ask what the hell was going on. It was bordering on cruelty, but now I know she was weighing me up, measuring my strength of character, testing my loyalty.

And now I know enough to know I'd do exactly the same in her position.

Eventually she smiled, as if I'd passed the test, and from her rucksack she produced one of those big drink flasks which has two cups in the lid. She poured two cups of coffee and as I took mine she added a drop of whisky from the bottle on the table to her own.

"The whisky isn't Eurof's, I presume," I said. It would be very old if it was.

"Frank's," she said. "We leave a bottle here in case anyone needs a little nip to warm up. You don't need any. You're younger than me, you've got enough bad habits already, and it's not cold enough for you to need some yet." I wondered how cold it had to get, because it wasn't particularly warm in there.

The silence fell again. I knew there had to be a reason why she'd woken me up at the crack of dawn and brought me here and sooner or later she'd tell me what was going on and until then all I could do was wait.

I looked around and noticed all the little ways in which the place needed work. It seemed a shame to let it fall apart. With a bit of work it could have been a great little hideaway or one of those quirky holiday lets people pay a fortune to stay in. If the island was tidied up a bit as well, that is. I wondered why, since she was obviously such a good businesswoman, she hadn't done more with the island.

When the coffee was finished she put the cups back onto the flask and said, "Well, that's about long enough I would think."

"Long enough for what?"

"For you to smell a little like everything else here. You have to have a familiar smell if he's going to trust you."

"Who?" I asked.

"Come and see," she smiled. It was the first proper smile she'd given me in over twenty four hours and I took it as a hint that things weren't as bad as they had been.

We went outside and sat on the steps, Joan with her rucksack beside her. "He knows to meet us here," she said quietly. I just nodded. The vague sense of gangster terror had evaporated but this still wasn't making any sense. I just had to sit and go along with it. Whatever it was.

You forget how cold wood can get. Or at least I had. A nip of the whisky would have been useful. My legs and bum were getting cold from sitting on the steps and the cold in the air was sinking into the rest of my body, as if it was a weight all around me. The silence didn't help. It reminded me of when we were in chapel at school and the nuns would give us killer looks if we even thought about speaking, and God help anyone who started to giggle.

Eventually she took some Kendal Mint Cake from her rucksack and passed me a bit. We nibbled it quietly and it was somehow oddly warming.

After what seemed a ridiculously long time we heard a rustling and then saw movement amongst the undergrowth on the opposite side of the clearing.

"There he is," she said quietly.

"Is that the pig Duncan and I saw?" I whispered.

"Wait and see," she said.

And then we heard the snuffling, the same sound I'd heard when I was there with Duncan so it was definitely the pig. Or whatever.

From her rucksack she produced a Cornish pasty. I almost laughed when I saw it because it seemed so ordinary and at the same time so incongruous to carry Cornish pasties over to the island and I wondered where she'd got it from. She looked at me as if she knew what I was thinking while she broke it in half.

Then she made a weird snuffling noise of her own and threw half the pasty across the clearing. I have to say if you'd ever met my grandmother you'd have been as surprised as I was by her making this ridiculous and slightly vulgar noise. It was not the sort of thing anyone would expect her to do. It seemed to come from somewhere between her nose and throat and sounded as if she was having enormous difficulty trying to sniff a lump of blue tac up one way and down the other.

Frankly it was fairly disgusting.

There was a pause and then another movement in the undergrowth. She made the snuffling noise again and this time another one came back across the clearing in response. Then all was still and quiet again. Nothing happened.

Nothing happened for a minute. As we've already established a minute can be an incredibly long time and I think this might have been the longest minute of my life. I was holding my breath again. Then I noticed a face amongst the undergrowth on the far side of the clearing and had no idea how long it had been there. It might just have appeared but it could easily have been there for a minute or two and I just hadn't noticed. I knew immediately this was what I'd caught a fleeting glimpse of when I was with Duncan and it was the same creature I'd seen when I'd been walking around the lake. But it wasn't a pig. It wasn't anything like a pig.

"Hello, boy," she whispered and snuffled again. "Come and have your pasty." He sniffed the air and caught the smell of the pasty. When he saw it on the ground he moved towards it and I saw him clearly and properly for the first time. He was about the same height as a pig but longer and thinner. His skin was medium brown with a speckled coat like a seal's. He lumbered forward like a cross between a seal on dry land and a hoppy, happy puppy. It was a lollop. Silly word, but I've never found a better one for it. He lolloped.

"What is this?" I asked quietly.

"This, my dear, is the La'lun."

"I thought I was the La'lun."

"You're a la'lun. He's *the* La'lun."

He lolloped towards the middle of the clearing and stopped to look at us. He had a sharper, darker face than a pig or a seal would have, a longish head more like a dog or wolf but with small ears set into the side of his head, and the big dark glassy eyes of a seal. He looked straight at me for a moment. He wasn't bothered about Joan, but he wasn't sure about me.

Then he remembered the pasty and decided I wasn't important. He wolfed it down and then looked at Joan as if he knew she'd have more. She held out the other half and he lolloped over to her. I noticed his strong legs and webbed feet and saw that his pelt was lighter on the underside. The lolloping movement seemed almost comical but his legs seemed perfectly designed to shift between swimming in water and hopping through the undergrowth. He was big, strong and looked heavy. I reckoned if he'd jumped on us he could at least crack a few ribs and give us a nasty bite.

But he wasn't going to do that. He sat at the bottom of the steps looking up at her like a soppy dog. She held the pasty out and he ate it from her hand, gulping it down without once looking away from her and it wasn't distrust that made him watch her so closely, it was affection. Affection which went both ways, because when I looked from him to her I saw the calmest, happiest expression I'd ever seen on her face. All the warmth and affection grandparents are supposed to have for their grandchildren seemed to be focussed on this strange but strangely wonderful creature. When he'd finished she held out both hands to show there was nothing else. He licked them both to get the last of the flavour and then she placed one hand on the top of his head. It looked like a priest giving a blessing but to this day I'm not sure who was blessing who.

"Just one hand," she whispered to me, still looking at him. "He doesn't like two for some reason. He likes the crown of his head stroked gently like this," and as she did so he cocked his head a little to one side and closed his eyes slightly.

After a minute or so she stopped and lifted her hand away. "Right then boy, that's enough for now," she said. "I'll see you in a day or two," and with that he turned round and lumbered off into the undergrowth as if he understood what she'd said.

"Shall we go?" she stood and picked up her rucksack. I didn't want to. I could hardly believe what I'd just seen and I didn't want to break whatever spell had been cast."Can't we stay?" I asked.

"That's it for now. He has to get used to the sight and smell of you, and that will take a few days at least."

"We could come back later," I suggested, and I really wanted to, but she shook her head.

"If we want him to trust you we have to take things gradually, step by step. We have to be patient. In the meantime we need to go home and warm up."

We retraced our steps through the island and back to the boat. From that point on my whole world was different. I walked, rather than ploughed, my way back through the overgrowth, hardly even aware of it. The water seemed smooth and calm and the boat seemed to take no time at all to ride back across the lake. The next thing I knew I was walking through the back door of the house and could smell breakfast being prepared.

14

After we'd changed out of our boots and jackets I sat on the sofa in the dining room while Joan was on the phone to someone and Frank was laying the table and bringing the food through. I was in a state of shock. I felt quiet, subdued even, but at the same time I had a million and one questions running through my head and Frank could see that from the look on my face.

"You look slightly gobsmacked," he said as he brought the plates through.

"I am," I said.

"All will be revealed!" he said with that twinkle in his eye as he disappeared for the final time into the kitchen. When he came back a moment later he'd taken his apron off and Joan came back into the room just as he sat down.

"There, now," she said as she joined us at the table. "I've done all the business calls I need to make this morning, I've left a voicemail for your mother and now you have my undivided attention for as long as you need it."

They say breakfast is the most important meal of the day, but maybe you have to have done something like climb a mountain, or abseil down the outside of a sky scraper, or gone out in a small boat on a freezing cold lake on a freezing cold morning and come face to face with a creature only a handful of people even know exists before you can truly appreciate that. I couldn't believe how hungry I was, and even though I wanted to ask all sorts of questions and know all the answers and everything else all at once as soon as I started eating I couldn't help but tear through a plate of bacon, sausages, black pudding, eggs, tomatoes, mushrooms and hash browns followed by a pile of toast with marmite and peanut butter and then some more toast with marmalade and about half a dozen cups of coffee and half a gallon of orange juice really all a bit faster than is good for you. It was only when I was coming to the end of the toast I realised they'd been quietly watching and laughing about me while they ate their breakfasts.

Frank stood up to pour Joan yet another cup of coffee and clear the plates away. "Better now?" he asked. I nodded, my mouth still full of toast.

"Right then," he said as he piled things onto a tray. "I'll clear up while you two catch up," and he disappeared into the kitchen.

"So, where do you want to begin?" Joan asked. I swallowed the last of the toast – you can imagine how she'd have reacted if I'd spoken with my mouth full. "Obvious first question: what exactly is that creature?"

"He's an Afanc," she said, and could see from my face I was non the wiser. "In modern Welsh it means beaver but in days gone by it was a creature from Welsh mythology, a terrible lake monster. As far as we know he's the last of his kind anywhere. He came here nearly sixty years ago with two older ones, who've both since died."

"They're in the graves by the cabin," I realised and she nodded.

"That's why I said there's 'no one' buried in those graves," she smiled. "I was teasing you. I meant 'no one' as in no person. He's the last of them, he was the smallest. Hence the La'lun."

Inwardly I breathed a sigh of relief. At least my grandmother wasn't a real Godmother. Not in the mafia sense, anyway. Then I asked, "If he's a creature from Welsh mythology what's he doing here?"

"We found him when I was there on holiday."

"Who's we?"

"Frank and me. We're very distant cousins, third removed fourteen times over or something like that, and I was spending the summer at his home." She paused, and smiled at the memory. "As I'm sure you've already noticed, if a young man is interested in you they try to attract your attention by showing off in some way."

"They sent me to an all girls school," I reminded her in as innocent a voice as I could manage. "I have no idea about such things."

"Don't lie," she said flatly. "It's an insult to both of us. You know perfectly well what I'm talking about."

"Like peacocks with their feathers," I said and she nodded.

"Frank had obviously taken a bit of a shine to me and so every night, when it got dark, he'd try to frighten the living daylights out of me with tales of ghosts and monsters, dead warriors and bloody battles. I told him he was being silly and I wasn't frightened but he carried on anyway and so eventually I gave him a challenge: prove that at least one of your stories is true and I'll stay with you for ever. And at the time I meant it."

"And you've been together ever since?"

"In a way, yes."

"You were an item?" I couldn't believe it – I'd only ever thought of him as cheery, happy Uncle Frank.

"Well up to a point," she said. "But not exactly. We were until he went off to Oxford and I met your Grandfather. But your Grandfather died quite young, as you know."

I nodded. "I never met him," I reminded her.

"It's a shame," she said. "He'd have adored you." I think that was possibly the warmest, most Grandmotherly thing she'd ever said to me. "So after your Grandfather died Frank moved in here to give me a hand and he's been here ever since.

"Anyway, I digress. After I'd issued that challenge Frank took me to meet Eurof, who was a bit of a local character, as they used to say. A bit of a hermit. He lived in a crannog, which is like a hut on stilts on the edge of the lake. Frank thought if anyone could convince me the stories were true it would be him and told him about my challenge. Once Eurof had stopped laughing he said if we absolutely promised never to tell anyone else he'd show us something really special.

"So of course we promised, and he took us round to the far side of the lake. There were hundreds of trees all the way down to the water and it was completely deserted. He told us to go and sit some way away while he sat down on a fallen tree trunk. 'They know my smell,' he said. 'If they smell you first they won't come near.'

"He took a Cornish pasty out of his pocket, and after what you saw me do I'm sure you can guess the rest."

"But there were three of them then," I said, just wanting to make sure.

She nodded. "Over the next week or so we got to know each of them and they got to know us. Eventually they trusted us enough to let us feed them and stroke them. Their pelts are unbelievably soft. There's more than one loathesome wretch that passes for a human being who'd like a coat made from that stuff."

"So if that was in Wales how come they ended up here?" I asked.

"Ah!" she said, and took a deep breath. "The more time we spent with Eurof the more we realised we wouldn't be able to keep our promise. He knew he wasn't going to live for ever and was worried about what would happen to the afancs after he'd gone. You see, at the time the local authorities were trying to build up tourism in the area and the lake was becoming popular for water sports. Sooner or later someone was going to discover them and that would be a disaster, so we had to protect them."

"So what did you do?" I asked.

"Frank and I talked about it for days. Eurof seemed to think we'd be able to take over after he died, but how could we? Eventually we couldn't see any other way out but to tell Frank's mother. And then we had to tell Eurof what we'd done. I'll never forget the look on his face. It was a mixture of anger, frustration and betrayal. He didn't say anything for a few minutes and he didn't do anything, but the look on his face had us rooted to the spot. We were too scared to even run away. And of course it didn't end there because Frank's mother had to tell his father.

"You see, lies and secrets are similar in a way. You can't tell a single lie. It's just not possible. Sooner or later that lie has to be backed up by another, which in turn has to be backed up by another, and before you know it you're stuck in a web of lies you've spun for yourself and can't get out of. And, in the same way, when you break a promise the consequences ripple through the rest of your life. It's like when you drop a stone into a pond and watch the ripples spreading outwards. You have no control, you just have to wait and see what the consequences are. We felt bad about what we'd done and we felt awful when Eurof actually told us how he felt. But then Frank's father suggested we move them up here."

"But how did you manage that?"

"It wasn't easy, but if you're determined enough almost anything is possible." She finished her coffee and then continued. "The reason I was staying at Frank's in the first place was because my parents had just bought this house and were having all sorts of work done to it before they moved in. They'd rented a cottage to live in while the work was being done but it was tiny so they packed me off to stay with Frank's side of the family."

A young girl abandoned by her parents and dumped on relatives.

This was beginning to seem like a family habit, but I didn't say anything.

"But then we got a postcard from Rome and it seemed they'd dumped me at Frank's at least partly so they could go on holiday."

"That was mean," I said.

She shrugged and said, "Holidays abroad were very expensive in those days and they probably couldn't have afforded to take me as well. And anyway, I wouldn't have wanted to traipse around the Colosseum and the Vatican and all that sort of stuff at that age. I was quite happy at Franks."

"So while they were away this house was empty?" I asked.

"Apart from the chaps doing the work," she nodded, "and they were going home every evening and not working at the weekends. My parents had already shown Frank's parents photographs of the house, the lake and the surrounding area so we knew it would be perfect for the afancs, *if* we could get them here," she paused as Frank came in from the kitchen.

"That's how the army got involved," he said as he sat down next to Joan.

"The army?" I wondered if this was another wind up, like the stolen lambs. "There were barracks not far away," he explained. "Still are, actually, they train in the Black Mountains. One of the soldiers was a friend of my father's, so they hatched up a plan together and within days it was all arranged and everyone was happy, even Eurof. Four soldiers came up here one weekend and camped on the island while they made the clearing, built the cabin and put up the 'No Entry' signs. Then the following Friday morning we all went down to the lake before dawn and the soldiers turned up with a huge open backed lorry with a tarpaulin cover. They had nets and Eurof had pasties. Lots of them. One by one they came to eat the pasties and one by one they were caught in the nets and taken up to the lorry. There was a sort of wooden cage big enough to hold the three of them quite comfortably and Eurof squashed up onto the back and stayed with them all the way up here."

"But they can't just have driven off from an army base with a great big lorry," I said. "Surely someone would have said something?"

"You'd have thought so," Joan nodded, "and I did wonder about that myself. While they were fastening up the sides of the lorry I asked one of them and I'll never forget what he said: 'We do everything our masters tell us, but we don't tell our masters everything we do.'"

Frank took up the story again. "Once they were off we followed in the car. It took most of the day because there weren't many motorways in those days, so by the time we got here the builders had gone off for the weekend. We backed the lorry down to the shore so anyone watching would think it was a boat being delivered. Eurof took the afancs over to the island one by one in the boat, they settled in quite happily and he liked it so much he lived there for the rest of his life. Came across for a hot meal and a bath a couple of times a week and he was as happy as a pig in muck."

"Which was sometimes what he smelt like," Joan pointed out.

"And he was happy just to live on the island?" I asked.

Joan nodded. "He must have been about ninety when he died. There'd been quite a storm and we were worried the cabin might have been damaged. We found him curled up on the bed, must have died in his sleep. He looked so peaceful, so happy."

"He was," Frank said.

She nodded. "He'd done what Voltaire said everyone should do."

"Who?" I asked.

She sighed, but I think it was more for show than anything else. "Voltaire, you ignoramus. Eighteenth century french writer and philosopher. Do they teach you nothing of value in school these days?"

"Probably not," I said.

"He wrote a story called 'Candide' in which a character suggested if everyone tended their garden the world would be a better place."

"What about those of us who haven't got a garden?" I asked.

"He was speaking metaphorically," she said, in a slightly withering tone. "If you haven't got an actual real garden there will still be something else you can choose to look after, to protect, and to do so will do you good and at the same time do the world some good. That's what Eurof did."

There was something about this idea that appealed to me. It seemed logical. If everyone did what they could in their own lives to look after their family and friends and the things in their life, then somehow it would all stitch together and the world would be a better place. I've thought about it often and to me it makes a lot of sense.

Joan continued, "When this house was finished and my parents moved in we had to tell them about the afancs, so again the secret spread a little further, but we kept it as close as we could. The warning signs worked a treat and we put it about that we'd found the island to be dangerous and it was best to stay away. Of course, now that you know the secret has spread a little wider…"

"Does my mum know?"

"Of course."

"My dad?"

"Don't be silly."

"What about Chris and Denise?' I asked.

"They don't know, and they mustn't," she said. "I like them but we can't let everyone in on this."

"It's all very well telling a secret to someone you trust," Frank said, "but that person will tell it to someone they trust, who in turn will tell it to someone they trust, until eventually…" he held his hands open.

"Someone tells it to someone you can't trust," I finished the point.

"Always happens sooner or later," said Joan. "Which brings me to the next question: how much has Duncan seen, how much will he work out, and what will he do with what he knows?"

Duncan had been looming like a spectre at the back of my mind during the conversation. "Like I say, he thought there was a pig there," I told her. "He wanted to run some stupid competition to give it a name. But then he noticed the graves, and obviously he's more interested in them, but with everything else that happened we didn't get chance to talk much. And now he's gone back to Carlisle."

"To write up the story?" Joan asked.

"Not straight away," I said. "He'll have other things to do and he'll want to do some research first. That gives us time. The bigger he thinks this story is, the less likely he is to tell anyone else."

"He's young and keen," Frank said. "If he can't find a story he'll make one up."

"But there is a story," said Joan. "We need to stop him."

15

As long as Duncan was at work in Carlisle there was no immediate problem. He wouldn't tell anyone else what he thought was on the island because he didn't want to lose the story, and he'd have to let me know if he was intending to go back there again. I just had to wait to hear from him. I guessed, and could only hope, that he wouldn't have told Sarah much either.

Not being able to see Sarah for two weeks meant that I had more time to get to know the La'lun and go out on Tod's boat. Not at the same time, because Tod didn't go on the island much, even though he knew about the La'lun. He said he was too old to go ploughing through all that jungle and unless it was an emergency he'd leave that for the youngsters, by which he meant Joan and Frank. I persuaded them to take me every morning for the next couple of days, even though the La'lun wouldn't be expecting it, because it was good for him to get to know me. And me him. And then after breakfast I'd walk round to Tod's to go out on the lake with him.

I couldn't tell how much older Tod was than Frank and Joan. He seemed just as sprightly and active as they were, although he was retired so probably had an easier life than they did. His wife had died years before and he was left rattling around in a big old house that looked out across the lake with a huge garden full of Rhodedendrums. A younger couple, Charlie and Catriona, lived in part of the house and "Did" for him, as he called it. Catriona did the cooking, cleaning and shopping while Charlie looked after the house and the garden and occasionally drove Tod around, a bit like a chauffeur but without the uniform. It seemed a comfortable life, if a little dull, and I think he was glad to have something new to do in teaching me about the boat and the water. He even tried to teach me to fish but even now I haven't got the patience to sit for hours when I could just nip to the fish and chip shop.

It was fun, and I learned a lot that still comes in handy now and again, but spending more time with older people gradually made me aware of something that left me feeling a little uncomfortable. They were elderly, there was no denying it. Yes, they were fit and active and kept themselves busy, but I began to look at them the same way they must have regarded Eurof. These were the people most responsible for the La'lun. What was going to happen if he outlived them?

There was still no news about my dad. Mr Clemence had gone mysteriously quiet and Joan made a few comments about him lying low and running up his expenses. I spoke to mum a few times and it was hard work keeping her cheerful. I didn't talk about it much with Joan because I think she was getting cross with Mr Clements and I didn't want to say anything that might make things worse. Plus I think she was as concerned as I was about how my mum would cope if dad didn't come home, and that was something I really didn't want to have to think about.

Frank and I were sitting on the cabin steps one morning waiting for you know who to show up and while we were waiting my mind wandered over everything that had happened since I got here. The people I'd got to know, the things I'd heard and learned, the fun I'd had, the art work I'd done, and I was struck by how, now that I knew about the La'lun, everything somehow made more sense. I felt as if I'd been brought here by some force much more powerful than me and this was where I was meant to be. This was what I was meant to do, and even if my dad didn't come back we'd find a way of making things work. Knowing about the La'lun, and getting to know him, was somehow making me stronger.

Eventually he came lolloping out of the undergrowth and, as usual, he stopped to look at me for a second but then remembered I wasn't a threat. He ate the pasty out of Frank's hand and went off quite happily without even giving me a second look. It felt like he was deliberately ignoring me, and I felt a little hurt. That might seem stupid, but trust me: it isn't.

Frank could sense my disappointment. "We're making good progress," he said. "He accepts you're there, that's a big step forward." It didn't seem like it to me, but Joan said the same thing when we got back again.

Each time we visited we stayed a little longer so that he got more used to me and as we left the house early on another cold morning Frank handed me the rucksack. "You can be pasty queen this morning," he said.

When we got to the clearing I threw half of it towards the far end and after a minute or so he came snuffling out. When he'd eaten the first half he looked at Frank expectantly and Frank nodded towards me. The Lal'lun saw the other half held out in my hand and hesitated for a moment. "If he doesn't come right up to you throw it half way," Frank whispered. "He might not be ready for you to feed him just yet."

But I really wanted him to be ready for me. I held the pasty out in my hand and spoke softly, almost whispering to him. "Come on, sweetheart, you know I'm not going to hurt you." We looked at each other, deep into each other's eyes. I smiled. I nodded my head gently. "Come and get your pasty," I whispered. I could see the hesitation, not just in his eyes but in his body. His limbs were ready to move towards me but he still wasn't quite sure. I didn't want to throw the pasty. I wanted him to know he could trust me. I wanted to know that he knew he was safe with me. I wanted him to take it, but I could see he wasn't going to.

"Give it to me," Frank whispered.

"No!" I snapped at Frank before I even knew I was going to and the sudden noise made the La'lun turn away and lumber off back into the undergrowth. "Oh, shit!" I said, again too loudly.

"You have to be patient," Frank sighed and he was right. Sometimes, when you want something so much, it's difficult to be patient but that's exactly when you have to be. I know that now. I didn't then.

But the next day was better. This time he ate the first half and turned to look straight at me rather than Frank. He knew I had the other half. I held it out in my hand and he took another step forward and then stopped, waiting.

"Come on, boy," I said. "You know it's okay." But he sat looking at me and I realised he was testing me. This was a battle of will. He wanted the other half but he wanted it on his terms and I knew if I dropped it this time he'd know he was still in charge on his island.

As soon as it landed on the ground he leapt forward to hoover it up and then grunt-snuffled his thanks and went off. It was a moment that changed my whole life. I realised that you can't impose your will on another creature, all you can do is either frighten it into submission, which obviously I wasn't going to do, or you had to build trust between the two of you and that means accepting them on their terms and respecting them. By giving in I'd shown that I accepted him as he was and now he could accept me.

Joan had breakfast waiting for us when we got home and I was so excited by what had happened I was telling her everything as if she'd never seen it herself. She sat listening with a gentle smile on her face and I realised the extent to which things had changed between us. That look in her eyes was a mixture of warmth and – more importantly – trust.

A couple of days later I went with Joan. He didn't mind me throwing him the pasty when I was with Frank but when Joan was there he was only interested in her. I tried holding out half of it but he just looked at her until I grudgingly handed it back and then he'd come right up and eat it out of her hand. It was frustrating and I wanted to try feeding him once more.

"I don't have any more pasties," she pointed out as he snuffled back off out of the clearing.

"Can we go back and get some?"

She sighed and said, "Let's try something else," and she wiggled a bit closer to me on the steps. "Copy me," she said and made the snuffling noise. She got it spot on, I really couldn't tell the difference between the noise she made and the one the La'lun made. But when I tried it sounded so bad she laughed out loud. "Don't laugh at me," I said, although I was beginning to laugh myself. "It's not easy and you're not helping!"

"Have another go," she said and did it again to show me.

"You sound like my dad snoring," I pointed out.

"It's similar," she said, "but do it from lower down in your throat."

I tried again. She laughed again. I tried again. "That's better," she said. The fourth time, maybe the fifth, I started to get it. "That's it," she said. "Do it again." So I did it again. "Louder." I did it again, louder, and we waited and nothing happened. "One more try and then we go," she said. I tried once more. I listened. I listened so hard and everything was so quiet that I could actually hear the blood pumping around my head.

And then I heard it. A little further round the clearing than it had been before, a little more to my right, and when I looked I saw movement in the undergrowth. Then he came out into the clearing and looked straight at me. I held my hand out, even though he could see there was nothing in it, and when I snuffled again he came lolloping across the clearing towards us and came right up to me and sniffed my empty hand.

And then he licked it.

And I fell in love with him there and then.

He's not the most gracious and elegant of creatures on dry land, and he's not the most beautiful creature I've ever seen by a long chalk, but I felt humbled to be in the presence of such a rare and special creature who had deigned to accept my presence in his world. I sat mesmerised as he licked my hand and when Joan whispered, "Stroke his head" I came out of the dream I was in and stroked the top of his head and the back of his neck. She was right, it was so smooth and soft I don't think I'd ever felt anything quite like it, and as I stroked the back of his neck he rolled his head to make the most of it, just like a silly puppy would have done.

My eyes welled up with tears because I was so happy and so proud and so honoured and if you, dear reader, don't understand that and have no idea of what I'm talking about then you have to go and find your own La'lun, something you feel that way about, and then you'll know. Other people don't count. There isn't a human being on the planet who can make you feel like that because we're the same species. Even a baby doesn't count because although it's so utterly dependent on you at first eventually it grows into another person, another human being. When you have a baby, or even a pet, you're bringing something in to your life and your world. This was completely different – this was a creature letting me into his life, his world.

Look hard enough and you'll find your own La'lun somewhere. You might have to learn to sail, fly, swim underwater or go into space. You might have to risk your life and maybe more than once but – believe me – when you find it, it will be worth it. You'll never be the same person again.

You'll be alive.

Eventually he'd had enough. I could have stayed there happily all day but he decided there was something more interesting to do somewhere else and lumbered off to find it. I watched him cross the clearing and disappear into the undergrowth and I watched where he'd disappeared for a while.

Eventually my Grandmother broke the silence. "Quite something, isn't he?" she asked and I couldn't speak because I had the biggest lump ever in my throat. I just nodded, and she put her arm around me and kissed me on the forehead. "Come on," she said, looking at her watch. "We really do have to be going."

16

That was when my painting became even more abstract. I was trying to capture my feelings and relate what had happened without actually painting the La'lun, for obvious reasons, so what ended up on the paper and canvass got more and more splodgy and splattery and for the first time in my life I knew it was exactly what I wanted. It was right, and it was good, and if no one else liked it I couldn't have cared less, that was fine by me.

I also researched Afancs. Apparently they were supposed to be wild monsters who lived in lakes and the only way you could subdue them was by having a beautiful maiden sing to one to lull it to sleep and then tie it up. And then – surprise! surprise! – when it woke up it would be pretty wild. Well, duh, you'd be pretty wild if someone did that to you, wouldn't you? The creature of legend bore little resemblance to the creature I was getting to know, and I came to the conclusion that stories were like secrets: something happens when they spread. When you tell a story it sends out ripples as it gets told and retold and spreads around the world, and with each ripple the story moves further away from the truth so eventually you're just left with a version of the story and no idea what the truth actually is, or was.

Which brings us back to Duncan.

Sarah's two weeks' grounding was almost up when he finally phoned me. I knew Sarah would have passed on my message and I didn't want to badger her about it because I didn't want her thinking there was more to it than there was, but I wanted him to phone so when he finally did I was annoyed with him.

"You owe me breakfast," I said as soon as I heard his voice.

"A 'how are you?' Would have been nice," he replied.

"Where've you been?" I asked, and instantly regretted it. He'd think I'd missed him.

"Busy," he said, deliberately vague.

"I wanted to talk to you but I couldn't use my phone."

"Aww, did little Camille get grounded by her rotten horrible Granny and Grandad then? Awww diddums!"

"If Joan hears you calling her 'Granny' she'll grind you into dust under her heels, and you know full well Frank's not my Grandad."

"Okay," he sighed apologetically. "Let's start again shall we? Hello. How are you?"

"Fine," I said. "I've been busy as well. I had to go round to Tod's to apologise about the boat and he insisted on taking me out to learn how to use it properly."

"Aren't you the lucky one? I used to be scared to death of him when I was a kid. He was always threatening to tell our parents what we were up to."

"Which probably means you were up to no good," I pointed out. "He's lovely, but I can see how he would have scared you when you were little, timid little creature that you must have been. He's teaching me how to fish for pike."

"What's the point? You can't eat it."

"You can, actually, and it's delicious. You just have to be careful with the bones and know how to cook it. He catches one at a time in a net he drags across the bottom of the lake and Catriona cooks them for him. It's amazing what you can catch when you drag a net along the bottom of a lake, but anyway, how are you?"

"I'm okay," he said, "but a bit stymied. I lost my phone when we got tipped into the lake, which means I lost all my contacts, and when I got back to work it took me ages to find the USB I'd backed it all up on. And then they sent me over to Penrith for a couple of days to talk to a farmer who's just gone bust, and since I got back they've given me loads of really stupid piddling stuff to do so I've hardly made a start on the real story. How far have you got?"

"I'm not writing a story," I pointed out.

"Yeah, but you must have found something out.

"Nope," I lied.

"Did you mention the graves?"

"Nope," I lied again.

"You're not helping much, are you?"

"Nope," be fair – that one wasn't a lie.

"Well I did manage to contact the Land Registry and it seems your grandmother really does own the island."

"I could have told you that."

"Yes, but I had to check it. What I don't get is, who would have known it would be a good place to bury bodies? Ever since I was a kid people have avoided that place. I've asked around a bit but so far I haven't found anyone who's ever known anyone who's even heard of anyone who's ever been on that island, so it was bound to be completely overgrown and wild. So how would anyone know it would be a good place to build a cabin and dig graves?"

It seemed obvious to me that an island that was thought to be dangerous in the middle of a quiet lake would be a perfect place to dispose of a couple of bodies, but I wasn't going to tell him that. I tried a different approach.

"Unless they're all lying to you," I said in a mysterious sort of voice.

"Huh?" I was beginning to realise that although he was, on the whole, very clever he could also be pretty slow on the uptake sometimes.

"It is possible," I pointed out, "that everyone you've talked to could have been lying. They might all be covering for each other. Everyone in this part of Cumbria might be mass murderers, bumping off awkward or ungrateful tourists right, left and centre. Have you seen the look the waiters give you if you don't leave them a big enough tip? That's probably what happens… the whole island might be jam packed with the rotting corpses of miserable tourists who weren't generous enough with their tips. What we found might just be the tip of the iceberg."

"You're making fun of me, aren't you?"

"Or… another possibility is they're not telling you anything 'cos they don't like reporters."

"Why would people not like reporters?" he asked, as if he didn't know.

"Perhaps because they tell lies," I suggested.

"When have I ever lied to you?" he asked.

"You told me you'd buy me breakfast and you didn't."

"I haven't bought it for you yet," he said, emphasising the 'yet'. "Will Saturday morning do? I can't get home until the weekend. Or we could make it afternoon tea…"

"Please don't think that because I'm a girl I'd rather have cucumber sandwiches and fairy cakes than Black Pudding and Cumberland Sausage," I told him.

"I'll pick you up at nine. They serve brunch 'til noon."

"Make sure Sarah's with you. I'm not having her calling this a date."

Phone down. Job done. At least the first stage.

The next job was not quite as straightforward. It went something like:

"Hello Geraldine, I'm sorry we got off on the wrong foot."

"That's fine. Just keep out of my way and keep your mouth shut."

"Yes, Joan told me you might say something like that."

"She's a mind reader as well as a tyrant, then. The minute I saw your face I knew you were trouble."

"Ah, then it's you that's the mind reader," I pointed out, but she ignored me.

"Eurof was a wonderful old man," she said. "He was like a grandad to me. I've felt him looking down and keeping an eye on us all ever since he passed over, and it's not right that someone like you comes along and risks spoiling everything."

That was when I started to get suspicious.

"How old are you?" I asked.

"Twenty three, why?"

"Well by my reckoning Eurof died about thirty years ago, so how come you saw him as a grandad figure?"

"He's been in contact with me. My mother's a medium."

Ahhh, right… I thought. Here's where it all begins to make sense.

Now let's get one thing straight, dear reader: I am not prejudiced. You are free to believe whatever you want to believe in, that's entirely your right and I will fight to the ends of the earth to protect that right – as long as you're prepared to fight to the ends of the earth to protect my right to believe in whatever I choose to, thank you very much, because otherwise it doesn't work and the whole system falls down. (I've been reading Voltaire. You can tell, can't you?)

That said, I must confess I'm a little sceptical about people who claim to be able to talk to people they've never met and who died a long time ago. (I've also been reading up my history and apparently this got going in the nineteenth century and then really took off after the First World War when so many people lost loved ones like never before.)

Then again, with all that I've seen in my life and everything else going on in the world, who am I to argue? Who can say they have the answer when we can't even agree what the question is?

But I digress, as Joan would say.

I decided Geraldine would be a work in progress. I'd come back to her later.

After Duncan and Sarah.

17

"What is this place?" I asked as we got out of the car at The Howgate and walked across a packed car park.

"A by product of Foot and Mouth disease," Duncan said.

"Huh?"

"In 2001 there was a really bad outbreak of Foot and Mouth disease. It started with some farmer in Northumberland feeding his cattle with untreated waste."

"Sounds lovely," I said. "Just when we're about to have breakfast."

"We have better animal welfare standards here than anywhere else in the world but sometimes people cut corners to save money," he continued. "You should never cut corners over something like food."

"Remember that when you're looking at the menu," Sarah told me with a nudge.

Duncan held the door open for us and we went into a hall with big comfy sofas on both sides. Through the windows in a door to our left we could see the dining room, which was huge compared to the one at Joan's hotel. All the while Duncan was talking, barely pausing for breath. I could tell we were in for a full blown report, whether we wanted one or not. "The upshot was Cumbria got it worst, over eight hundred cases. Thousands of cattle had to be slaughtered and to try to prevent the disease from spreading the whole of the Lake District was pretty much closed to tourism. Farms, hotels, restaurants, cafes, they all suffered and loads went out of business."

A smiling waitress invited us to sit on one of the sofas until a table was free and handed us menus as we sat down. And still he carried on.

"When it was all over we needed the tourists to come back, and in case the weather was going to be rubbish they decided great food should be a big attraction. So on a wave of optimism new cafes and restaurants opened, new chefs arrived, farmers markets opened, and this is one of the newer, trendier hotels." He actually paused for breath at that point and looked around him. "I like it," he said, looking a bit smug as if he owned the place. Finally he was quiet while he looked at the menu. Sarah winked at me and mouthed "He's paying." As if I'd forgotten.

I could see why he liked it. It was warm and welcoming but at the same time managed to be cool, in the trendy sense rather than the uncomfortable sense. The dining room had bare wooden tables, comfortable chairs, and bare stone walls covered with huge photographic prints of views from the tops of the fells, taken by a mad man who gets up before dawn and climbs up in the dark so he's at the top of the hills ready to get the most dramatic shots as the sun rises. I'm not sure what Joan would have to say about that, so I didn't mention them.

The doors and windows were painted the same shades of green and grey Joan had at her house and the hotel. Joan's hotel's lovely – don't get me wrong – but the Howgate was livelier and I liked that. Joan's place is smaller so didn't have the same 'fun vibe', you might say. Later on, when she asked me what I thought of the Howgate, I said it was as nice as hers but in a different way. She knew exactly what I meant – surprise, surprise – but she wasn't offended, thank goodness.

"That lively 'fun vibe' can easily turn into something more trashy when it's full of the wrong kind of people," she said and I wondered, not for the first time, how she managed to keep her business going when she had such a distaste for so many of her fellow human beings. I also wondered how I'd managed to avoid inheriting the snotty gene my Grandmother seemed to have in such abundance.

Maybe I haven't. I'll leave you to be the judge of that.

The Howgate served the biggest and best breakfast I've ever eaten anywhere in my entire life, and it was so good it was difficult to talk whilst eating. But talk I had to, I was on a mission.

"So how were your parents after your dad took you home?" I asked.

"In case you'd forgotten I was grounded for two weeks," Sarah said. "Which made me even angrier than they were."

"You can't blame them for being angry," I said. "They were worried about you."

"They weren't as angry with him," she nodded towards Duncan.

"Oh, they were," he said, "it's just comes across in a different way when you're older and you've left home."

"So as well as boring us with your detailed account of the Foot and Mouth outbreak of 2001 you're going to patronise us as well, are you?" she asked.

"I'm just saying it's different when you're older," he tried to defend himself.

"Yes, thank you, Duncan, we get that," she said. "Doesn't make it any easier."

"Dad had a real go at me when you weren't around."

"Well so he should. It was all your idea."

"I know it was my idea," he said. "I thought it was a good one at the time. It just didn't turn out to be as good as I thought it might be."

"Does he always overstate the painfully obvious?" I asked.

She nodded. "Has done ever since junior school. One of the oh, so many reasons why I love him as much as I do."

In retaliation Duncan stood up and in one swift movement leaned across the table, took her face between his hands, and before she could react planted a great big kiss on her lips and sat down again. The people at the tables on either side of us smiled and there was definitely an 'awwww' from somewhere.

"For God's sake!" Sarah said as she wiped her face with her napkin. "You are so embarrassing!"

"Shut up and I won't embarrass you!" he smiled. This was turning into one of their sibling spats which wouldn't do anyone any good so I tried to bring the conversation back round to the matter in hand.

"Did they ask what we were doing?" I asked.

"Of course," Duncan replied.

"So what did you tell them?"

"I told them the truth. I was looking for a story."

I'd long ago reached the point where I didn't like that word 'truth'. Not in the hands of a journalist, anyway.

"So what did you tell them you found?"

"Nothing. I told them I was hoping to find Pine Martens but didn't. I didn't tell them about the pig because if I told them they'd tell other people and the story would be everywhere in no time at all. You've heard the phrase: a lie is halfway round the world before the truth has got its boots on."

"It wouldn't be a lie," I pointed out. "We did find a pig."

"We found a wild boar."

"You just said it was a pig," I reminded him.

"I thought it was a pig at first, but then I realised it was more likely to be a wild boar. And a better story, too."

"You mean a bigger, better, more sellable story?" I suggested.

"Exactly," he smiled. "That's what we saw, that's officially what the story will be until I've had chance to investigate further. And until I know more I'm not saying anything else to anyone. I don't want anyone snatching this story."

Inwardly I breathed a sigh of relief. Since Chris and Denise didn't know about the La'lun they couldn't have told Duncan and Sarah the truth, and Duncan didn't seem to have told his parents or his sister about the graves, which was the real story as far as he was concerned. This gave me a bit more time and space to work with. This could be manageable, I thought. But it would need careful handling.

"If I was a betting man," Duncan hadn't stopped and wasn't going to, "I'd put money on it not even being the only one. For all we know there might be dozens of them there. We only saw one but in all that undergrowth there could be any number of them, entire families of them."

"Gosh!" said Sarah, letting her head fall towards her plate. "This story could go on and on! And on… and on…"

"But there's more to it than that," he was ignoring her.

"Like what?" she asked.

"Well they're not pigs, are they?"

"No. You've just said. They're probably wild boar." She rolled her eyes upward.

"Yeah, but they're not, are they?"

"What are you on about?" she asked. "You just said they are, you're confusing me!"

"Not difficult," he said.

"Stop it," I snapped at the pair of them. "What are you talking about?"

"I'm calling it a wild boar for now but we all know it's not a pig or a boar because they can't swim like that. Whatever we saw on the island was most likely the same thing that rammed the boat and tossed us into the lake."

Not for the first time in my life – or the last, either – I felt as if something had just slapped me round the head as I realised I'd overlooked something very important. I'd been so afraid of the consequences of disobeying Joan after this all kicked off, and then got so wrapped up in getting to know the La'lun, getting him to trust me and learning to use a boat, that I'd almost forgotten about being thrown into the water. I'd more or less forgotten that it was the La'lun that had done that. That big lolloping creature I'd fallen so much in love with had very nearly killed me, and I'd completely overlooked that small point until now.

This was serious.

I'd assumed Duncan was more interested in the shallow graves. I had to change tack and jump in quickly.

"It was a current," I said. They both looked at me slightly oddly. "Joan and Frank told me that's why not many people go out on the lake. There are currents that can hit you quite forcefully. Tod showed me how to watch out for them but you can't always see them coming. We were just unlucky."

"How come we've lived here all our lives and never heard about this, and you come along and find out so quickly?" Sarah asked, ever so slightly suspiciously.

"You haven't lived by the lake all your lives. Tod has. Well, most of it," I said. "That's why you were both told not to go near the lake when you were kids. It's not just the island that's dangerous."

"We were told not to go near the lake because we weren't strong swimmers," Duncan said. "No one mentioned currents."

"Well they didn't need to if you weren't strong swimmers! It was enough just to tell you not to go there." I knew I was on thin ground. If he checked with his parents they'd say they'd never heard of the currents. I was going to have to bluff this one out. "Why do you think that lake is such a quiet area when the rest of Cumbria is such a tourist spot? Look around us – this place is heaving but I bet we're the only ones who've been on that lake." I was beginning to get through to them, although rather slowly. They were thinking about it, at least, rather than dismissing it out of hand. I had to keep going. "I mean think about it, what else could it have been? What we saw must have been some kind of boar, pig, whatever, probably cross bred with something else over the God knows how long they've been on that island undisturbed. But it must have been one of the currents that tipped us into the water." They were beginning to look convinced. "If we'd been hit by, I dunno, some Loch Ness Monster type of thing the boat would have been damaged, wouldn't it?" They nodded. "But it wasn't! It stayed upright after we fell in, and thank God it did because otherwise we'd have frozen to death before darling Sarah here could get help." I reached across the table and squeezed her hand. "I never did thank you for saving my life, did I?" I asked. "I owe you one." She squeezed my hand back and I thought I saw a slight welling of tears in her eyes. I felt bad for a second because I'd said that just to get round her but then I saw that I really did have a friend for life.

Duncan nodded and said, "You're probably right." Yay! I thought. Finally I've got through to him. "But even if it was a current that tipped us over and all we saw on the island was some sort of pig that doesn't explain what else we saw."

"What else did you see?" Sarah looked up, suddenly interested. My heart leapt, and for a split second Duncan looked surprised as he realised he'd said too much.

"Buried treasure and the ghosts of pirates, what do you think?" He said, but she knew him well enough to know the sarcasm was a cover.

"What else did you see?" she repeated and the look on her face said she wasn't going to be fobbed off. So he told her about the graves. "For God's sake, Duncan!" She almost yelled and he waved at her to turn it down.

"You can not tell anyone else," he spelt it out. "You have to promise me."

She looked at me and I nodded.

"All right," she said. "But you're a pair of idiots."

"It could be a big story," he reminded her.

"It could also be your last," she said and went back to her breakfast.

"At least we'll know what we're looking for when we go back," he said.

"Who's we?" I asked, although I had a horrible feeling I already knew.

"Well you and me, obviously, and Sarah if she wants to."

"No way!" she said so emphatically a bit of scrambled egg flew across the table and landed dangerously close to my plate. "Sorry," she said, and then added, "I'm not going anywhere near that island or anything on it."

"Which is exactly what someone wants you to think and say," he pointed out.

"And again you're stating the unbelievably obvious," she replied.

"I must confess I have similar reservations about going back," I said rather weakly. I was quite happy with him thinking I was utterly pathetic and girly after all.

"What's the problem?" he asked.

"It's dangerous, for a start," I said.

"No it isn't."

"Yes it is," said Sarah. "I don't care if you end up dead but Camille's my friend."

"The shallow graves are just the start," he said. "I've been thinking a lot about the whisky bottle. That suggests someone is either on the island or visits it frequently and I want to know who."

"What whisky bottle?" Sarah asked, and when he told her she said, "Right, that's it. You're not going and if you don't drop this stupid plan of yours I'm telling mum and dad the whole story."

"Oh, that's pathetic!" he snapped. He was cross and I was worried. I didn't want him to go back but neither did I want her telling anyone what we'd found.

"That's Tod's," I said. I don't know where that came from and when it did I didn't have time to think it through, it just sort of blurted out.

"What?" Duncan asked.

"Tod," I said. "He told me he sometimes goes over to the island for a bit of peace and quiet and he keeps a bottle of whisky there for when it's cold." Well that bit was partly true, I suppose, but Duncan didn't look convinced.

"So he knows we found the clearing?" I nodded. "Did he say anything about the graves?"

"No, and I didn't ask him."

"Okay," he said, thinking aloud, "The whisky is Tod's, fair enough." I was already assuming Duncan wouldn't ask Tod about it, but in case he did I made a mental note to prime Tod first. Joan was right, you can never tell just one lie. "But who built the cabin?" he wondered aloud.

"Joan and Frank, when they were young." There goes another, I thought. This is getting messy, even though they'd back me up on that one if needs be.

"Makes sense, I suppose," he nodded. "But what about the other things you can see from the cabin?" He wasn't even going to say the words 'shallow' and 'grave' in public any more in case anyone overheard. I thought this might crop up and I'd been racking my brains for the last couple of minutes trying to keep one step ahead with a plausible explanation: A couple of family pets? Why no markings? Dangerous chemicals? That would be another story for him to follow. So I did the best I could.

"Kids looking for treasure," I told him.

He looked at me for a second and then asked, "Really?" I nodded, perhaps a little too enthusiastically. "Kids don't go on the island," he said.

"These did," I argued. "Holidaymakers a couple of years ago. Two kids, brothers, one older than the other," I was getting into my stride. "Reckoned they had a treasure map from somewhere and took a boat over and started digging." I paused as I tried to read his face. "Geraldine saw them coming back from the island and got Frank and Joan onto the case."

"Why dig in two separate places so close to each other?" Duncan asked.

"Because they had the map!" I was starting to enjoy this. "They realised they'd measured it wrongly so they started again." I left the idea to sink in and watched his face closely. I realised I should have sorted all this out ahead with Joan and Frank, but they just assumed I'd be able to bluff my way out of whatever cropped up.

Duncan was looking straight at me but he wasn't seeing me, he was thinking past me and on to the island. I decided to push the point home. "There's really nothing there that adds up to a story," I said. "Unless you want to make one up." I don't know why I said that. I suppose it was a kind of challenge, to see if he was basically an honourable and decent human being or if he really would create a story out of nothing. I wasn't completely expecting the answer I got.

"Fine," he said. "I'll go alone."

"You can't," I said. I didn't want him going back without me keeping an eye on him.

"Who's going to stop me?"

"Okay, I'll come with you."

"I thought you said you didn't want to."

"I don't want to, but if you insist I have no choice."

"I can go on my own."

"No, you can't," I repeated. "The island is private property. The signs warn that trespassers will be prosecuted."

"It's owned by your Grandmother."

"Exactly! If I go with you we'll just get another rollicking and I'll probably never be allowed out of the house ever again as long as I live. Go on your own and she'll prosecute you."

For a split second he looked worried but then his face lit up. "That's something of a feather in your cap for an investigative journalist," he said with that same smug look he'd had earlier.

"Not if you can't pay the fine," I pointed out. "She'll call in your dad's debt. He'll go bust."

His face fell. "She wouldn't do that," he said without conviction.

"I wouldn't bank on it," I said. "They don't call her the Godmother for nothing.

18

So there we were, dear readers, early in the morning a couple of days later, back on the lake on Tod's boat, but with his permission this time. I told Duncan I'd cleared it with Joan and Frank but they were worried about how dangerous and uneven the ground was on the island so this would be our one and only chance. Frank was alongside us in his and Joan's boat and Joan, Sarah and the lovely Geraldine stood on the shore together watching as the recently refitted outboard motor on Tod's boat sped us across the lake.

This time we were tooled up for the job. We had thornproof jackets and trousers, gloves, walking sticks, knives, water, food. Well, I say food, it was Kendal mint cake, which apparently counts as food but even though I've eaten plenty of it over the years I'm still not convinced.

And cameras. Digital SLR cameras which cost a fortune and didn't just have the world's best lenses for still photography but also shot video in high definition. This time we were ready and whatever the island revealed would not escape us.

At least that was Duncan's plan.

Mine was slightly different.

Mine was to get him on the island, deeper into the undergrowth than we were last time, then trip him up to twist or break his ankle so he couldn't move. I'd set off to find help and get so 'lost' on the way back that by the time we found him he'd be dead.

Nah, not really.

Although there had been times in those few days when I'd been tempted. I'd spent a lot of time and effort gently trying to persuade him that it wasn't worth it, that it wasn't such a big deal, that it had to be wild boars we'd seen and a couple of wild boars stuck on an island would get maybe a hundred and fifty words at most in one of the national dailies as a novelty item, and that was only if he could produce a clear photo. And I stuck like a limpet to the story of the kids with the treasure map. The last thing I wanted was for him to start digging up dead afancs. Either way it wasn't going to be the big break his career needed.

In the meantime he was rushing around like the proverbial blue bottomed fly covering everything he was asked to by the paper all over the county while preparing for this trip without even telling them what it was really all about. I did worry that when they found out how much of their time and money he was wasting they'd just give him the sack and I did raise that prospect with him, but to no avail.

I tried everything I could think of to persuade him it wasn't going to be worth it and he might as well forget it, but he was like a man possessed. He just wouldn't let it drop. I even began to wonder if he'd worked out the truth somehow and knew exactly what he was looking for. I had no way of knowing until we got there.

Frank led us to another part of the island which he said was easier to land on and less overgrown. Of course it wasn't the place we usually landed, we didn't want Duncan to know about that. The plan was Frank would wait offshore in his boat in case of emergencies while Duncan and I explored the island. We waded through the water at the island's edge in wellies this time and when we got onto dry land changed into nice dry walking boots. No more squelching for the likes of us.

The sun was already quite high in the sky and it was getting noticeably warmer, but we couldn't even unfasten our jackets without being ripped to shreds by the thorns and brambles. We ploughed on for about ten minutes or so without seeing or hearing anything and then suddenly he called out, "Wow! Look at this!"

He was holding up an old wasp's nest. It was huge and horrible. Twisted around and around and in on itself it was head shaped and looked like one of those 'green men' you sometimes see made out of different fruit and vegetables, except that this was decaying, smelt awful and looked positively evil.

Nevertheless it gave me an idea.

"Hold it up," I told him as I looked through the viewfinder on the camera his paper had very kindly loaned me. I'd used something similar at school but this was much more sophisticated and way more expensive. I took dozens of photographs really quickly, walking around him to get it from different angles as he held it up beaming goofily as if he'd found valuable treasure.

"What else can we find?" I asked when I'd finished with that. I watched carefully where we were going as we ploughed our way towards the centre of the island and then I found something else that could be useful. "Look at this!" I called. It was a branch of a tree, about a foot long, which had dried and snapped off with a fork at one end. He laughed as I held it up. "What's so interesting about that?" he asked.

"It's nature's way of giving the V sign," I said as I handed it to him. "Hold it up".

"What for?"

"I'm going to create a collage of 'Our Day Out – the flora and fauna of the isle of pigs'," I said.

"Is that what we're calling it? The island of pigs?"

"Isle of pigs sounds better than isle of wild boars."

"Island of pigs it is, then."

"Isle of Pigs," I corrected him.

"As in 'Bay of Pigs', the disastrous invasion of Cuba by the USA in 1961?"

"Isle of Pigs, as in Isle of Dogs."

"As in where they buried all the dogs after the plague?"

"Okay, Mr clever journalist, you're a walking Wikipedia and we're all very impressed. You can stop showing off now." By then I'd taken about twenty photos of him holding it from different angles.

"If you're going to be rude to me you might not get off this island," he threatened.

"My uncle Frank's waiting for me, and he's bigger than you!" I said and stuck my tongue out.

"I'm not scared of your uncle Frank."

"Maybe not, but you're scared of my grandmother!"

Just as this was about to descend into childishness we both heard a rustling and he raised his hand as a signal to be quiet. I knew it unlikely but I'd been hoping not to hear that noise on this particular visit. Now that we had heard it it was time to put my plan into action.

We stood stock still for a moment and didn't hear a thing. The La'lun, for his part, was probably standing absolutely still and listening to us. And watching us. Then we heard it again and I pointed one way and Duncan pointed the other. He was right, of course, I was just trying to put him off the scent.

He set off in the right direction and almost as soon as he did so we could see the undergrowth shaking as the La'lun lolloped its way through. By then I knew the island well enough to know that he was heading for the clearing. Duncan was racing after him with me following as fast as I could.

We reached the clearing but there was nothing there. We stood still again for a moment and I was about to suggest we go when the La'lun's face appeared amongst the vegetation. Duncan pointed the camera and took a single shot. The clicking of the camera was enough to alarm the La'lun and he shrank back into the undergrowth. Duncan was about to race after it when I held him back by the arm. "Don't go," I said. "Come here," and I led him to the stairs outside the shack.

"What are you doing?" he asked with more than a note of irritation in his voice.

"Just sit and watch," I said quietly. We sat and after a moment I snuffled. He looked at me as if I'd gone completely mad but I shook my head to tell him to be quiet. I snuffled again and then I heard the reply. I guessed he could see me even though we couldn't see him and I held my hands out to show him that although I had no food with me I hadn't brought any harm either.

That was when he came into the open and stood in the clearing sniffing the air, obviously aware of Duncan's smell. He took a few steps forward then stopped and stared at Duncan. I'm not sure which of them was the most surprised. For a moment neither of them moved and then slowly, very slowly, Duncan raised his camera, focussed and took a sequence of photographs using the quick shutter release. The sound of the motor driving the shutter brought the La'lun to his senses and he shot off back into the undergrowth while Duncan was still taking shots of his backside.

When the La'lun had disappeared Duncan turned to me and said, "Well done. You managed to miss it completely."

"Huh?" I said and I realised he was annoyed because I hadn't taken any photographs. He thought I'd simply imitated the La'lun and when he came into the clearing that was just luck.

"You've got to be a bit quicker off the mark," he said. He was beginning to annoy me again.

"Doesn't matter now, you've got it," I said.

"I don't know if that's enough," he said.

"It is."

"I could have done with more."

"You've seen it for yourself, that's all you need," I told him.

"No it isn't."

"Duncan, you're not going to sell this to the papers."

"What? Why not?"

"Because you can't," I said. "I don't want you to."

"What's that got to do with anything?" he almost sneered.

"I'm asking you, please. Just forget the whole thing."

"Why? I don't understand."

"That creature is probably the only one of its kind anywhere."

"How do you know?"

I didn't want to tell him the whole story, the real story, because I knew he'd want to sell it. "I don't know, I'm just guessing. But even if it isn't, what right do we have to come over here and disturb it like this? What harm has it done us?"

"It nearly bloody drowned me," he pointed out. "That was no current in the water."

Fair point, I thought, but I said, "And what if it did? Can you blame it? We frightened it. There's probably been no one on this island for years and it's been left alone in peace, what right do we have to spoil that?"

Something shifted in his expression. There was a flicker of distrust. "You know that's not true. Tod comes here, you said so yourself." I'd forgotten about that. "If Tod knows about this I can get the story from him." I knew I had a choice there and then: add another lie or spread the secret. My options were running out. "Someone's been keeping this secret for a long time," he said. "If it's not Tod then it's someone else and whoever it is has not wanted anyone else to know about this." He was talking about Joan.

"Oh, Duncan, listen to yourself," I almost laughed. "That's conspiracy theory stuff. You'll be saying there's a crashed UFO here next!"

"The wonderful thing about conspiracy theories is they can never be disproved."

"Yeah, and the journalist who puts them forward is never taken seriously." Point to me, I thought.

"I've got the evidence," he waved his camera to remind me.

"Yeah, evidence that there's some poor creature who's been living here undisturbed for God knows how long and you're happy to blow that all away for just a few quid. What kind of person does that make you, Duncan?"

"I'm a journalist," he said in a quiet, rather menacing tone. "This is what I do."

"Look, Duncan, you really can't do this," I said. "If you've ever so much as given a quid to Greenpeace or whatever then you owe it to them not to do this."

"I have to do this," he was still speaking softly. I could see something in his eyes I'd not seen before. A glint of cold, sharp steel, and I didn't like it. "This could be a really big story," he said, "and it's mine."

I was beginning to understand why so many people say they hate journalists. I was beginning to hate this one. He really hadn't thought or didn't care about the consequences, he just wanted the story.

"What would happen if you ran this story?" I asked him. "There'd be journalists and tourists and bounty hunters and scientists all looking for a piece of this. Not just a piece of the story, a piece of the creature. They'd take it away for examination.

They'd prod it and poke it in a hundred different ways and experiment on it as if it was an alien of some kind. It would be terrified, and for what? It's the last of its kind so all we'd learn is that we frightened the last one ever to death."

"I've done a lot of work on this over the last couple of weeks," he said. "I know who to sell it to, and how. I promise you, Camille, with syndication rights around the world, advertising revenue from putting the story out on the web, this could easily bring us in at least a million. Net."

"A million pounds?" I laughed. I thought he was kidding.

Then I saw his expression and knew he wasn't.

"After tax," he nodded. "I'll split it with you, fifty-fifty. We need to find it again and get some good footage, but then we set up a limited company to manage the copyright and the licensing and put it out around the world and on YouTube. I promise you. Half a million each. At least. Think what you could do with half a million."

I was thinking of what I could do with half a million. That would change everything. I hadn't bothered to check the exchange rate that morning (I know, it was remiss of me) but even I knew that half a million pounds was more than half a million dollars. Half a million dollars would get my dad back. Half a million pounds would make everything all right.

But this wasn't what was supposed to happen. I was supposed to have talked him out of it and be back in the boat by now. Instead I was faced with an uncomfortable choice: side with Duncan, betray my grandmother, Frank, the La'lun, everything, but raise the money to pay dad's bail. I'd have my dad back. But Joan would never ever forgive me. And neither would Frank. And neither would the La'lun.

Or, I could give it one last go. Tell Duncan everything and beg him to keep it to himself. But that would be another way of betraying Joan. Deepen the lie or spread the secret. Either way was a betrayal, but in the end what choice did I have? If I told Duncan the whole story he'd be even more excited. He'd be like a Catherine wheel going off. And even if I could get through to him and he promised to keep it secret, how long would it remain a secret? At some point he'd be tempted to use it to further his career. And even if he didn't, how long would it be before he let something slip? Sooner or later he'd be in the pub with his colleagues, have one too many and blab. I had no choice. I had two options, and both of them involved betrayal.

But then I thought of a third.

"Okay," I sighed. "Let's do a deal. Leave this story alone and I'll give you something else instead."

"What?" his voice was a mixture of suspicion and contempt. Which was pretty much how I was feeling about him.

"A scoop," I said. "Something almost no one outside my family knows about yet, but it could grow into something really big. A major international diplomatic incident. And you'd be the one to break it."

"What?" he asked. I knew I'd aroused his interest from the tone of his voice.

"My dad's been arrested."

"Big deal. So what?"

"In Nicaragua. Central America."

"I know where it is, thanks. What's he doing there?"

"He's there on Government business. He's a spy."

"He's a spy," he echoed, slightly sarcastically. "Obviously I'd have to check that."

"But that's just it: you can't. What he was working on was so dangerous he went in totally under the radar and now he's been caught the British Government are denying they even know him."

"There are ways of getting this checked, you know."

"For God's sake just run with it! There's no point in checking it, you'll lose the scoop if you do that."

"I have to check it!"

"What the hell do you care?" I was almost shouting by this stage. "You're a journalist, you just want a story! I've handed you one on a plate — what more do you want?"

"It has to be true. I have to check it."

"Never let the truth get in the way of a good story, isn't that what they tell you?"

"This is nonsense, you're telling me all this just because you don't want me to write about that… that… pig thing we've just seen."

"You're right. I don't."

"Well it's too late, I'm afraid."

"Okay," I said. Time for plan B. Actually by that stage it was probably more like plan F. "Write up this story and it's the end of your career before it ever really gets going."

"What do you mean?"

"I've got your phone. The one you lost in the lake."

"How did you get that?"

"It got caught up in the net when Tod and I were out fishing."

"Well it's no good to you, it's been in the water. It's ruined."

"Not entirely," I smiled. "It's amazing what you can do with a bowl of dry rice. You take the phone apart, cover the bits completely with a load of rice and leave it for a couple of days. All the moisture in the phone is gradually absorbed by the rice. Hey presto – you're phone's as good as new!"

"That's theft," he sounded wounded. "It's not your phone."

"You can have it back as soon as we get to Joan's," I said. "I don't want it." He looked slightly confused, so I explained. "I've copied your phone's contents onto an external hard drive. All your texts, calls, photos, and all your contacts. All of them. Personal and professional. You write this story – ever – and every one of those contacts will see it's a lie. They'll know the story's a fake, and they'll know you're a fake."

"The story's not fake. It's real, and they'll know."

I shook my head. "I have photographs with today's date embedded on them of you, on this island, mucking about with a wasps' nest that just so happens to look like a creature's head and a branch that looks suspiciously like a trotter or a claw of some kind. I also took a few others of you that you weren't aware of. Enough to make it look as if you just might, possibly, perhaps, ever so slightly, have faked the whole story. You know you didn't. I know you didn't. But the rest of the world doesn't know. All it needs is just a little seed of doubt, a tiny, tiny crumb of a question, and they'll never know for sure if they can trust you. About anything. Ever. So they won't."

I think I saw it coming before he even knew what he was doing. I saw the rage in his face and as he leaped towards me I rolled forward off the steps and out of the way. It hurt when I landed on the uneven ground and rolled over but it gave me the time I needed to get away from him. I ran out of the clearing and minutes later I was through the undergrowth ahead of him and waving to Frank.

"We're done!" I called, and he waved back and started up the motor.

Duncan arrived a moment later as I was changing out of my boots and back into my wellies. "That camera's on loan to you," he almost shouted. "It's not your property. Give it back to me NOW!"

I must admit I was quite pleased with the way I managed to continue changing my footwear with one hand whilst handing him the camera with the other without even looking at him. "Ha!"

he said as he snatched it out of my hand. He opened up the little compartment where the memory disc was housed and tipped the camera to one side slightly as he pressed the button to eject it. Nothing fell into his hand. He looked again and then shook the camera and then looked at me. I was looking at him by then and smiled my sweetest smile. I saw his lips start to form a word that was probably unspeakably rude or nasty but then he changed his mind and stopped. I wished I could have taken a photograph of him just at that moment. He looked really stupid with his mouth half open like that.

"I suppose you think you're clever," he said.

Dear reader, you have no idea how tempted I was to say something like 'Actually, yes I do, because I took the memory disc out of the camera without you even noticing and obviously it's somewhere about my person but God help you if you try to find it, boy, because if you lay a finger on me you really won't get off this island alive.' But enough damage had already been done. I didn't want this to get any worse. I still wanted Sarah as a friend and, perhaps, in time, Duncan as well.

I got into the boat first and started up the motor. I wanted him to know that I was in charge. We crossed the lake to where the others were waiting and as Frank and I pulled the boat up towards the boathouse Duncan went over to the others and I heard him say, "There's nothing there. It was a complete waste of time."

I caught Joan's eye and she gave me a smile.

Geraldine made us all a nice cup of tea.

19

By this stage I knew my Grandmother well enough to know that she was pleased with me. Not exactly proud, perhaps, but pleased. Well probably a little proud of me as well. We had dinner at the hotel that evening – me, her and Frank – and there was a bottle of champagne to begin with and then some pretty good food. But it was a bit odd because we couldn't tell anyone what the occasion was.

"So, go on, then. What are we celebrating?" Terry asked as he opened the bottle.

"Nothing," Joan shrugged her shoulders dismissively.

"You asked for the best champagne we have in the cellar," he pointed out. "There's got to be a reason for it, you're too mean for there not to be!"

I don't know who shrieked loudest, me or her. Frank just laughed his big laugh and said to Terry, "Be very careful, young man, you're not irreplaceable, you know!"

"Oh, but I am!" he said. When he'd filled our glasses he put the bottle in an ice bucket and disappeared into the kitchen. He came back a moment later and said "I've checked with Perry. He says if I go, he goes." We looked towards the door to the kitchen, where Perry stood in his whites shaking his head and mouthing "No I did not!"

The whole evening was like that. Just really silly and happy and even though I'd always thought Joan and Frank got on well, that night they just seemed happier and funnier and better together than ever. I suppose that's the thing about secrets. You have to keep them, but when you can share them it's a load off your mind, and sharing that secret with me without having to tell the rest of the world was a load off theirs.

While we were eating dessert (sticky toffee pudding, since you ask, which just about every hotel in Cumbria claims to have had at least a hand in creating but might actually have originated in Canada) Joan's face took on a more serious expression.

"There is one thing we perhaps need to draw to your attention, dear heart," she said and I knew from the look on Frank's face this was something they'd discussed and decided to bring up that evening. "You're a part of this now, whether you like it or not, so you will have your part to play."

"What can I do?" I asked.

"The La'lun is only comfortable with Frank, Me, and now you."

"What about Geraldine?" I knew she'd been on the island a few times.

"Not so much," Joan shook her head. "I'm not sure why."

I could have suggested a couple of reasons but one thing I was beginning to finally learn was when to keep my mouth shut.

"We're not sure how old he is," Frank said, "but the others lived a good long while and the chances are he will as well."

I know I can be a bit slow sometimes, but this time even I realised what they were getting at. "Yeah, I was wondering about that," I said. "So, if you die within the next few years..."

"Neither of us have the slightest intention of doing so, I can assure you," Joan said. "We're both as fit a fleas so it's not likely to happen any time soon. But when we do shuffle off this mortal coil you're going to have to step up to the plate."

Now, like I said, I'd been thinking about this myself when I was spending time just with those two and Tod, so on the one hand it shouldn't – and didn't – come as a shock. But on the other hand I suddenly found my mind racing forward like it's never really done before. All those things adults talk about and warn you about and get excited about on your behalf because it's all still to come and it's all so very exciting and you put to the back of your mind because you don't think it's relevant to you, at least not now, not yet, all that came rushing up to the front of my mind. Suddenly I could see the rest of my life set out before me.

By someone else.

Some. Thing. Else.

And I wasn't sure I liked the idea.

"I'm fifteen," I reminded her. "I haven't even done my GCSEs yet."

"I know," she nodded.

"I don't even know which school I'll be doing them in," I pointed out and again she nodded.

"Then there's A levels. University, Gap Year, Art School, I dunno, whatever I decide to do. I've got my whole life ahead of me!" And when I said it out loud I realised exactly what that hackneyed old phrase really meant, as if you can only truly understand it when you can see it being taken away from you.

"You just have to hope that Frank and I live long enough for you to get all that done before you settle down to whatever it is you're going to do," she said.

"But whatever it is I end up wanting to do, it will have to be something I can do from here," I said. It was partly a question but mostly an acknowledgement of what was now inevitable.

She nodded again, and said, "But look at it another way: you'll have the house, and this hotel. The house is mine and Frank and I own the hotel between us. He doesn't have anyone else to leave it to, so you're having somewhere to live and a comfortable, steady income handed to you on a plate. How fortunate is that?" Fair point, I thought. At least it meant I'll never starve. At least as long as I don't make a complete pig's ear of everything. But I'd be stuck here, and whilst I liked being here for now the idea of being here for ever wasn't what I had in mind. "And let's face it," she smiled, "this is the most beautiful part of the country." It was if she could see exactly what I was thinking.

"Yes, it is. I love it here," I said. "I just don't know if I want to be tied to this place for the whole of my life."

"Some of us are born to greatness, some of us have it thrust upon us," Frank said.

"I've heard that," I nodded.

"Well congratulations, kid," Joan said. "You've just had this thrust upon you, and that's that. If you don't like it you shouldn't have disobeyed my instructions in the first place. But you did, and this is what's come of it. This is, if you want to look at it this way, your punishment. Disobeying my instructions means you now have a responsibility. This is your garden. So tend it."

"I know," I nodded.

I did know.

I understood.

"And let's face it," she started again, and obviously wasn't going to let this drop until she was sure she'd got the point across. "There are some people your age who've had far greater responsibilities thrust upon them, and they don't come with such a comfortable life attached."

"I know all this," I tried to explain, "it's just that I didn't really want my whole life mapped out for me quite so soon."

"Oh stop whining, child! So you want to do what everyone your age does these days: finish your 'A' levels, go around the world to places everyone else your age visits, do the things everyone your age does and then go off to University where you'll waste two and a half years in bars and clubs and then work like hell for the last six months in the hope of getting a good degree and a job at the end of it.

"Well the good news is you'll probably get to do all that before I pop my clogs, if you really do want to be just like everyone else, but if you don't get to do all those things then so what? When you come to live here you'll be doing something no one else in the whole world will be doing. Isn't that worth something? You're going to be doing something really useful and truly wonderful, and if no one else knows you're doing it – again, so what? You'll know, and that's what matters. Most people never get the chance to do something this special. Or don't take it when it's offered to them."

"You're right," I said.

She was.

I knew.

"Good girl," she said quietly and called for another bottle.

We'd gone in Joan's Land Rover but as the evening wore on it was obvious we were going to have to get a taxi back. Needless to say Brian, the taxi driver, was a friend of theirs so I wasn't expecting any money to change hands at the end of the journey.

And neither was I expecting what was waiting for us when we got home.

As we approached the house Brian suddenly slowed down and said, "Are you throwing a party or something?"

Frank said, "Don't be so touchy – we'd have invited you if we were."

"Then what's all this?" Brian asked and we saw about a dozen people gathered outside the gate.

"Can you pull over, please, Brian," Joan said. It was difficult to see in the dark. They were just dark shapes for the most part, occasionally lit up by moonlight. After a minute she said, "Some of them have got cameras."

"They look like reporters," Brian said. "What are they doing here?"

I think we all knew the answer to that.

At a stroke what had been a lovely evening became the other possibly worst day of my life. I wanted to scream. I wanted to cry. I wanted to shout and scream and kick. I felt so betrayed I wanted to shout and scream and kick Duncan. I wanted to kill him. I knew exactly how Eurof had felt. I didn't dare look at my Grandmother.

"Brian, can you drive past them, take us right around the lake and then in through the back way?" she asked.

"Your wish is my command," he said as he stepped on the gas. We got a better look at them as we drove past and they were definitely reporters.

"Take it steadily please, Brian," Joan said and then whispered to me, "Keep an eye on the lake, look for boats."

We looked but we couldn't see. It was dark, and there was no obvious activity on the lake. I felt numb. More than that, I felt empty. I felt as if my insides had been ripped out and the ground I stood on had been pulled from underneath me. There was suddenly nothing. I'd lost everything at a stroke. We were half way around the lake before I plucked up the courage to face Joan and when I did she was looking at me. I couldn't think of what to say so I didn't say anything. I just looked at her and hoped she'd understand. And when she took hold of my hand, shook her head and silently mouthed "It's not your fault" I knew she did. That should have made me feel better, and in a way it did, but only in a way.

It took about half an hour to drive the whole way around the lake and then Brian drove in through the gate at the side of the garden so we could go in to the house through the back door. As we ran out of the car and up to the house they started calling out to us, asking for 'any comments' and 'just a quick word' but Brian did a pretty good job of distracting them by reversing back up to the gate rather quickly and noisily so some of them had to leap out of the way. The last thing I heard as we closed the door behind us was one of them swearing at him as he drove off.

I'll give them credit for one thing: they don't give up once they've smelt blood. As soon as we were in the house the phone rang and it was one of them. Frank told them politely it was past their bed time and then disconnected the phone. Then Joan's mobile went – it was the only one that got a signal inside the house – so that had to be turned off as well.

They were there all night. I know because we watched them all night. The best view of them was from my bedroom window so we sort of set up camp there, taking it in turns to go down to make drinks in the dark and carry them up without turning the lights on. It was like being under house arrest. Or being besieged. They made sure to stay just beyond the boundaries of the house so they weren't trespassing, but it was still a horrible feeling having them there, not knowing what they might do.

By the early hours of the morning we'd come up with the only battle plan that might possibly work: absolute denial, backed up, if necessary, by the photos I'd taken of Duncan with the wasp's nest. The island was off limits to them unless they were happy to risk prosecution, so all we could do was hope none of them saw the La'lun in the water. As Joan had said earlier, if they did it would be the Loch Ness Monster all over again.

As dawn was breaking I suddenly had an idea. "I've got all Duncan's contacts on my computer," I said. "Why don't I contact them all and tell them it's nonsense, a non story?"

Joan shook her head. "Best not to say anything," she said. "If you say one word to them they'll twist it into a story. We have to sit this out for as long as we can and then just flatly and simply deny it. The less we say the less they can twist."

Frank cooked breakfast as if it was a normal day, and we ate it as normally as we could whilst being aware of the crowd outside. We'd drawn the curtains, as much so that we couldn't see them as to stop them seeing us, but while Joan and Frank were washing up I peeked through the curtains and was dismayed to see there were even more of them. When Joan saw for herself she said, "All right, flat denial as agreed. If we don't talk to them sooner or later they might start making things up."

Almost as soon as she turned her mobile on it rang again. She answered it and I could hear the voice at the other end although I couldn't hear what was being said.

"Yes, that's me," she said. Then she turned to face me with a wide eyed exaggerated expression and said "Yes, he's my son in law." I wondered what my dad had to do with all this when her phone bleeped to tell her she had a text. Several texts, in fact. "No," she said to the reporter, "I'm afraid I have no idea what you're talking about. Good day." She ended the call and almost immediately the phone rang again so she put it onto silent while she looked at her texts.

"What's my dad got to do with it?" I asked.

"Hang on a minute," she said a little absent mindedly as she scrolled through her messages. "These are nearly all from your mum." She dialled my mum's number and got an answer almost immediately. "Hello, darling – " I heard what sounded like my mum giving her a telling off. "Yes, they're here as well. They've been here all night so we turned the phones off." She paused while my mum rattled on for a minute and then said, "Just don't say anything. Not a word. They can sort things out and if we say anything we might mess it up. Yes, fine. Do what you have to. But don't talk to the press. I'll phone you later." She ended the call and turned to me. "Well," she said, almost laughing. "This isn't what we thought. It's your father they're interested in."

"What?" I asked. "But how did they -" and I didn't finish the sentence because of course I realised how they'd got the story. Duncan must have told them. Even though he knew my dad wasn't a spy he'd still gone and sold the story. "Oh, fair enough," I said to Joan. "I can't blame him. I told Duncan my dad's a spy who's been arrested in Nicaragua and the government's not helping him out."

"Well why on earth did you tell him that?" she asked as Frank came in from washing up. She turned to him and asked, "Do you know what she's gone and done?"

"I think I might have an idea," he said.

"I had no choice," I defended myself. "He was going to run with the whole story about the La'lun, I had to think quick and that was the best I could come up with." Joan started laughing. "What's so funny?" I asked.

"You told Duncan your father had been arrested?"

"Yes."

"And you told him it was because he was a spy working for the British Government on something so secret that when he was caught the government denied even knowing him," she'd stopped laughing but was still smiling broadly.

"Yes, like I said, it was the best I could think of – "

"And that's what's so funny," she said. "It seems it's more or less the truth!"

"What?" By now you'll have realised that this part of my life had contained one or two shocks and surprises but this one could almost take the biscuit. "I made it up," I repeated.

"That's the lovely thing about stories," she said. "Just because you made it up doesn't mean it isn't true. It turns out he was doing something for the Foreign Office and the Nicaraguan Government working together and it was so hush – hush that the Nicaraguan Police knew nothing about it and not many people in the Foreign Office knew either. That's why he's been in prison for so long with such a ridiculous bail set."

I tried to think this all through. "But Duncan must have sold -"

"I don't think Duncan even tried to sell the story," she said. "It seems he just sent it everywhere in the hope that someone would pick it up. And they all have, which might, in the short term, make things a little more complicated."

"I need to talk to him," I said as I ran up stairs to get my phone. Which was turned off, of course, and when I switched it on again I couldn't even get a signal. I screamed in frustration and ran back downstairs shouting something like "If you want me to live here full time when I'm older you're going to have to get a bloody phone mast set up in the garden!" Just as I picked up the landline phone it rang again. "Go away!" I said and put my fingers down on the receiver buttons and lifted them up again quickly to dial Sarah's home.

"It's me," I said when she answered. "I need to talk to your brother."

"Can't."

"Don't try to protect him," I told her. "It's too late for that."

"I'm not protecting him, he's not here."

"Then where is he?"

"On his way back to Carlisle."

"Why's he going back to Carlisle?"

"Probably to get hung, drawn and quartered by his editor."

"I need to talk to him."

"No you don't."

"Yes I do, you don't know what he's done."

"He hasn't done anything. I did it."

"What?"

"I sent out the story about your dad, not Duncan. He told me about it and said he'd checked with some friends and they reckoned it was probably true but he'd be deep in the mire if he ran with it. So I sent it out instead."

"Why?"

"You want your dad back, don't you? I reckoned this was the best way. Even if the press can't run with the story now they will be able to at some point and that will put pressure on the Government to get things sorted out. And judging by the call I've just taken for Duncan I'd say it's worked. It was an editor asking how he got the story because the Foreign Office has just agreed to some of it. I think your dad might be on his way home."

"Really?" I felt as if I could cry.

"Job done. Who cares if a few officials or the odd journalist gets hurt? Point is, your dad's coming home, hopefully."

And he was.

And the version the press eventually ran with bore little resemblance to the truth, which hardly surprised me by then, but as Sarah said, "Who cares? They got a story and you got your dad back."

And even Joan was a little more tolerant towards him. He settled down and got himself a nice sensible job with a proper salary and at the end of the holidays I started my new school, and for the next few years my life was just as I always expected it to be: Exams; Gap Year; Art School Foundation Year; Art School proper, make a living as an artist. Quite a good one, actually. Living, I mean – I'm still not sure how good I am.

And every holiday I'd be back up at Joan's and everyone thought it was because I was such a loving granddaughter. But she knew why. I knew why. And now you know why.

And now I'm here all the time, and I'm writing this because I might be the last one to be able to. Tod died a couple of years ago, Frank died last year and it was Joan's funeral last week. Geraldine's over in Canada – she fell in love with one of the hotel guests and more or less eloped – so now there are only three of us here who know the whole story.

Me, Duncan and Sarah.

Duncan worked it out, eventually. We had to tell Sarah, even though we didn't really want it to spread to even one more person. Sooner or later she'd have worked it out for herself so we told her and she laughed like a drain for about a week as she kept going over events and remembering things and finding that so much more made so much more sense when she knew.

It was funny watching Duncan at the funeral. He was on one side of the church, shaking hands with people as they left and thanking them for coming, while I was on the other side doing the same. All back to the hotel for a bit of a shin-dig afterwards. Terry and Perry are still there and they put on the best spread anyone's ever had at a funeral. Joan had left instructions for Champagne to be served to everyone, and I think we nearly emptied the cellar.

So now the secret's spread a little further because you, dear reader, know as well. But you won't know until it's too late for you to do anything with it. You won't be reading this until after the La'lun has died. Until then the secret has to stay safe with just the three of us. Sarah won't breathe a word because she's still my best friend, and Duncan won't tell anyone.

I know he won't.

I know I can trust him.

It's one of the reasons I – eventually – married him.

Acknowledgements

I caught my first glimpse of the La'lun many years ago and I'd like to thank Andrea for helping me find him again after so long. Thanks also to James Atkinson-Thompson, Jem Butcher, Ellie Dawson, Robert Dinsdale, Ryan Kelly, Sabrina Scolaro, Elaine Sharples and Jo Thompson. They know what for.

A lot of what's in this book actually did happen, some of it didn't. You'll have to decide for yourself which is which.

JNH